"Do you know what I thi

Emma mused

He raise his brow. "No."

"I sometimes think that it wou

to be a man's mistress."

Both his brows went up.

"I don't mean mistress in the sense of a married man's lover. I mean that sometimes it seems like it would be a pretty good deal to be a man's kept woman. Have him pay my living expenses in exchange for on-demand sex." She grinned. "Hey, I'm horny anyway. It would kill a couple of birds with one stone."

"Could you *do* that? Emotionally?"

Could she really do it? Not unless it was someone like Russ, whom she wanted to sleep with anyway. She made a show of tapping her fingertips along her jaw and tilted her head, looking up at the ceiling as if considering. "I'd have to like the guy or at least respect him. And I'd have to find him physically attractive." She slid a glance toward him and smiled wickedly. . . .

Praise for bestselling author Lisa Cach

"[A] delight."
—*Publishers Weekly*

"Ms. Cach's writing is open, bawdy,
and laugh-out-loud funny."
—*Romantic Times*

ALSO BY LISA CACH

A Babe in Ghostland
Have Glass Slippers, Will Travel

Available from Pocket Books

THE EROTIC SECRETS OF A *French Maid*

LISA CACH

POCKET BOOKS

New York   London   Toronto   Sydney

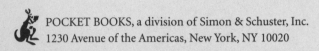 POCKET BOOKS, a division of Simon & Schuster, Inc.
1230 Avenue of the Americas, New York, NY 10020

Library of Congress Cataloging-in-Publication Data is available.

ISBN-13: 978-1-4165-1330-8
ISBN-10:   1-4165-1330-2

This Pocket Books trade paperback edition February 2007

10   9   8   7   6   5   4   3   2   1

POCKET and colophon are registered trademarks of
Simon & Schuster, Inc.

Manufactured in the United States of America

For information regarding special discounts for bulk purchases,
please contact Simon & Schuster Special Sales at 1-800-456-6798
or business@simonandschuster.com.

To the men of the Seattle Adult Hockey League

The Erotic
Secrets
Of A
French
Maid

One

Emma Mayson wrenched on the parking brake and hoped her incorrigible Honda Civic wouldn't roll down the steep driveway, into the side of the multimillion-dollar lakefront house below. It would suck equally badly if her car hit the Jaguar parked in front of the garage. She yanked harder on the parking brake, making sure her souped-up little car wasn't going anywhere. Then she popped the hatchback and got out to fetch her buckets of cleaning supplies, sponge mop, broom, and other housecleaning miscellanea.

The house below was an example of Northwest Modernism, probably built in the 1960s by Roland Terry or one of his emulators. Horizontal planes were punctuated with wide gables that reminded her of Northwest Indian lodges, and under those gables and planes were walls of plate glass. Emma felt a nudge of respect for the person who had bought this house rather than one of the new McMansions or pseudo Mediterranean villas squatting like false royalty around the lake.

Someday she, too, might design the type of building that becomes a landmark in the decades to follow, her name synonymous with a new architectural style. Someday, she might design houses and buildings as remarkable as this one—instead of cleaning them. They hadn't mentioned in graduate school that the market was flooded with aspiring architects, and that more than a year could go by before finding an internship position with an architecture firm.

A year in which to go through what remained of a small inheritance from one's grandmother, and to begin receiving repayment statements from one's student loan services.

She sighed and propped her broom and mop against the bumper. As she hoisted her canister vacuum out of the back, the wind tossed her dark ponytail across her face and into her lip gloss, where it stuck. She tried to pull it out and, distracted, bumped into the broom, which clattered to the pavement, knocking over a bucket. The bucket started to roll down the driveway, careening drunkenly toward the Jaguar with a peculiar determination, as if its whole white plastic life of janitorial humiliation had been waiting for this chance to take a chip off an expensive car.

As Emma yelped and raced after it she saw two men appear at the front door of the house.

"Shoot, shoot, shoot!" she said under her breath as the bucket rolled toward the car with murderous pleasure. She lunged and stopped it inches from the side of the Jaguar, but thudded against the side panel herself.

"Ow!"

The bucket sat motionless and innocent, looking up at her with its wide-open brim, daring her to challenge it.

"Are you all right?"

The voice drew her gaze, and she met the hazel eyes of a thirtysomething man. He had brown hair and stood a little under six feet tall, broad-shouldered and trim. His regular features were unremarkable except for the intensity behind them: his precisely focused look pinned her like a bug to a board, demanding an answer.

Emma pushed away from the car and stood straight. "I'm fine, thanks."

His eyes swept over her as if looking for signs of damage and then came to rest again on her face. He didn't say anything more, and Emma felt an awkward tension building.

She smiled brightly. "No harm done! And the bucket chase woke me up; I didn't have my coffee this morning."

A hint of smile breathed across his lips.

The other man scooted past them to examine the panel of the car, rubbing the spot where Emma had hit. He was about the same age as Hazel Eyes, but shorter and with a thin, wiry build,

"Kevin, knock it off. Your car's fine," Hazel Eyes said.

"I can't help it! I just know something's going to happen to it."

"I told you you should buy something older, with dents already in place. You're going to make yourself crazy trying to keep that thing perfect."

"It's a beautiful car," Emma said to Kevin.

His toothy smile revealed braces that glinted with sunlight. "There!" he said triumphantly, to his friend.

"He bought it as a chick-magnet," Hazel Eyes said.

Emma chewed her upper lip as a silence descended. They seemed to be waiting for her to comment, as if, as a representative of womanhood, she could settle the dispute. "Er . . . I'm sure it will impress a certain *sort* of woman."

"Ha! Gold diggers!" Hazel Eyes declared.

"Maybe," Emma admitted, and saw the crestfallen expression on Kevin's face. "And maybe it will attract women who are looking for a stable, established sort of man who will be able to afford sending their children to private schools."

"Country club matrons." Kevin scowled at his Jaguar, some of the love clearly lost.

"I forgot your name," Hazel Eyes said abruptly to Emma. "You're the one my sister hired for me, aren't you?"

She blinked, realizing this must be Russell Carrick—the workaholic entrepreneur who, according to his sister, Pamela, had been sleeping on the same unwashed sheets for the past year and didn't know a toilet brush from a hair brush.

"Emma Mayson," she said, smiling at Pamela's rants on his bachelor habits. "Your new housekeeper."

"Russ Carrick. Pleasure to meet you." He gripped her hand firmly and Emma's heart skipped a beat as energy zinged straight from his hand down to her loins.

He scowled for reasons unknown and released her hand, then turned to his friend. "Kevin, I have to show Emma the house. I'll see you at the office inside an hour. Make sure everyone is ready for that conference call: I don't want any screw-ups this time."

Ooh, he was bossy. Emma's native sense of mischief reasserted itself, and she wondered what he was like in private, with a girlfriend, and whether she called him pet names like *pookie* or *snookums*. She had to bite back another smile, picturing his reaction to such endearments.

"It should go better this time," Kevin said, getting into his car.

"It has to." Russ turned back to Emma. "I'm afraid this is going to be quick."

Emma imagined him saying the same thing before having sex, and grinned.

Russ's eyes narrowed.

"Lead on," she said innocently and gestured toward the house.

Russ muttered something unintelligible and led the way.

Pamela, whose house Emma also cleaned, had told her that Russ was in software. Like two-thirds of Seattle, it seemed, with the other third divided between Boeing, Starbucks, and Amazon.com.

Russ stopped at the front door to flip open a keypad mounted on the outside wall. "Pamela did a background check on you and assures me that you have rock-solid references, so I'm going to give you the code to open the front door. I usually won't be here when you come."

"Okay." She listened to his terse yet thorough explanation of the locks and alarms and then at his prompting, stepped forward to try it herself. He stood close, watching her fingers tap in the sequences.

"Well done," he said brusquely when she finished without error.

She murmured a noise that could be construed as thanks only by someone not listening closely. She hated being praised for brainless tasks, as if she were a dog who had sat on command. It was one of her personal quirks—or flaws—and had caused her grandmother to scold her for having too much pride.

"Is there a problem?"

"No, no problem."

Russ gave her an assessing look, then seemed to dismiss the issue.

Emma followed him through the foyer and into the main part of the house. *"Holy monkeys!"* she gasped.

The foyer's dark matte stone floor turned into a gallery-like hall ten feet above the living room. The room below was thirty by fifty feet, and its long wall was two stories of glass that let in a sun-filled view of lake and sky. Even on a dark rainy day, the room would feel bright. The furnishings looked professionally chosen, in neutral tones of gray, tan, and pale blue, echoing the view beyond the glass. A dining table long enough for a castle's great hall dominated one end of the room, with bronze chandeliers hanging above it.

The room was stunning. Magazine-worthy. And except for one oversize chair with a rumpled throw blanket wedged into a corner and a stack of newspapers and several coffee mugs on the floor beside it, the room looked completely unused.

"I hope you don't expect me to do windows! Jeez, I'd never want to leave the house if I lived here; I'd just sit in front of the windows watching the water all day. Do you get tempted to do that?"

"I'm rarely here during the day. The kitchen is this way." He headed off to the right, down a flight of open stone stairs and through a door into a stainless steel and polished wood kitchen.

Again only one small area showed evidence of human life: the corner of the counter where a small bag of coffee sat before a built-in espresso maker. A cutting board with a knife and hints of pink grapefruit pulp was between it and the sink, which held three days' worth of cereal bowls and spoons.

"You're okay with emptying the dishwasher, aren't you?" he asked.

"Of course. Funny how no one likes putting away clean dishes, don't you think? Just like no one likes changing the toilet paper roll."

"I don't have time for it."

Okay, so he wasn't one for idle chatter. Emma mentally shrugged her shoulders.

She followed him through the house, listening with only half an ear, her eyes taking in the details both of his ass, and of the house. She was so tempted to lay her palm over one rounded cheek and give it a squeeze. When not evaluating his butt, she evaluated the feel and flow of the rooms, guessing at where the constraints of construction had forced the architect to make less artistic choices, and admiring the places where form and function existed in elegant symbiosis.

Neither man nor house resembled his sister, Pamela, and her home, she with her frosted blond hair and her house with its warm—albeit faux—Mediterranean style and the scattered detritus of three small children.

"This is my room," Russ said, entering a bedroom with French doors leading onto a small deck.

It was obviously the master suite, and Emma wondered why he hadn't called it "my bedroom" or "the master bedroom," but "my room." Like a child who only has one room to call his own, instead of the entire house.

The only pieces of furniture were a queen-size mahogany canopy bed with green velvet curtains tied back at the posts;

a bench at the end of the bed, covered with discarded clothing; and a white iron bedside table that looked like it had been pirated from a set of patio furniture. The articulated metal lamp clamped to it would have fit better on a college student's desk than in a multimillion dollar house like this.

"I didn't have time for the decorator to finish this room," Russ explained, apparently realizing that the bedroom demanded an excuse for its condition. "She kept asking me to make choices. Showing me pieces of fabric and photos of chairs. Doorknobs. Area rugs. I didn't have time for it."

"Ah." Emma was beginning to get an idea of just how important time was to this man, although he didn't seem in a hurry to finish their tour. Instead, he stood frowning at the unsatisfactory space before him.

"Do you want the sheets changed once or twice a week?"

"Once, I suppose. I don't know. How often do people change them?" he asked, turning to her.

She shrugged. "Depends on your personal taste and your . . ."

"My . . . ?"

"Activities."

He stared at her, and for a long moment she was afraid she'd crossed a line. Then his gaze brushed quickly down her body before he turned his attention back to the half-furnished room. "No time for that, either."

He was either one heck of a busy man, or he had some serious problems with his priorities.

Not that she was one to talk, Emma thought. It had been a year and a half since she'd had sex, and there were times she thought she'd happily tackle any passing young male and put him to the good use that evolution intended. But evolution had also made her too picky and cautious to act on the urge; her health and welfare demanded more care than one-night stands with strangers, however tempting the notion.

Still, there were many nights when she yearned for an anonymous man to take her six ways from Sunday and not stop until she was too exhausted to even sigh.

Despite her ravening urges, though, Emma had set the pursuit of serious romance aside while she hunted for a position with an architecture firm. She wanted to be actively moving forward on her career path before she got involved with a man, since she wanted that man to be someone who wanted to be involved with an ambitious professional woman—not a man who wanted to be involved with a housekeeper. An educated housekeeper, a housekeeper with dreams, but a housekeeper nonetheless.

In her vision of herself there was Present Emma: the woman she was now; and there was Super Emma: the woman she intended to become. Super Emma had her hair professionally trimmed once a month, her makeup subtly and flawlessly applied, her clothes chosen with conservatively arty taste, and she was involved with a cultured, intelligent, sophisticated man who treated her like the precious flower she occasionally wanted to pretend to be.

"I'm sorry about the smell," Russ said, jostling Emma out of her reverie. They were in the master bath. "It's bad, I know." He was swiftly tossing soggy clothes off the top of the hamper into a laundry basket.

Emma wrinkled her nose as the odor of old sweat hit her nostrils, reminding her of high school gym. "I assume you'll want me to wash those."

"*These?* Hell, no." His intimidating air was replaced by embarrassment. "I don't expect you to touch these."

Emma moved closer, curious. "What happened to them?"

"Nothing. They're my Puck Skins."

"*What?*"

"Long underwear for ice hockey. And my towels and stuff. I know they're horrible; don't touch them."

"You play hockey?"

He pulled a towel off a bar and spread it over the top of the laundry basket. "In an adult amateur league. It's a good workout."

Emma looked again at his nicely rounded ass. "I'll bet it is."

Maybe Russ Carrick's life wasn't so unbalanced after all, if he made time for sports. But she wouldn't have guessed that someone like him would play *ice hockey;* wasn't that for jocks?

And what was with the embarrassment over his sweaty gear?

Emma followed him through the rest of the house, growing intrigued with her new employer. She didn't see any signs of a woman, or of a male lover either, if that was where his interests lay—although she doubted it. There was no extra toothbrush, no signs of cooking meals for someone, no photo of the happy couple, no special effort to make the home inviting for a romantic visitor. No package of condoms on the patio furniture nightstand, and only one pillow on the bed, the others thrown into a pile on the floor. That, more than anything, confirmed that Russell Carrick was alone in this romantic world.

Maybe he didn't want to add the distraction of a woman into his busy life. A few minutes in the shower every morning and his needs could be met by Mr. Hand.

Or maybe his standards were too high. From his comments to his friend Kevin, it didn't sound like he had an overwhelmingly positive view of women.

Maybe he had loved and lost. Or loved and been royally screwed over. Divorced, and still not over the pain?

"Any questions?" he asked abruptly as they returned to their starting point in the foyer.

Dozens, but none she could ask.

Maybe he was single because women found him unapproachable. If it hadn't been for his reaction to his dirty Puck Skins, Emma would have wondered if the guy was capable of emotion.

"I can also pick up groceries for you or cook meals to be

reheated later, if that's a service you're interested in," she offered on the spur of the moment, inspired by his barren kitchen.

"Is that by the hour?"

"Either that, or we could work out a flat weekly rate," she improvised. She didn't shop or cook for anyone else; hadn't even suggested it. But suddenly, looking at Russ and his empty house and empty kitchen, she wanted to be there for longer than it took to scrub out a shower and vacuum.

Besides, she'd rather grocery shop and cook than clean. If he went for it, she might be able to drop one or two of her other houses.

He stared out the windows on the other side of the house, contemplating the offer. Doubtless he was doing an in-depth cost-benefits analysis.

It must be his intensity that she found attractive—besides that skater's butt and the hazel eyes. He didn't seem angry or bad tempered so much as extremely focused. He was probably difficult to work for, demanding perfection yet unwilling to repeat or expand upon directions.

He badly needed a woman in his life. Someone to draw out his softer side, his emotional side, and nurture it.

"You're a decent cook?" he asked.

"My mother trained me from the time I was old enough to hold a spoon. Do you have any favorite foods?"

"Anything hot."

"Temperature, or spiciness?"

"Both," he said with laconic precision. "I'll think about your offer and leave you a note on the kitchen counter with my answer, the next time you come."

"Okay. No pressure, I was just offering."

"Of course there's no pressure. I never do things I don't want to."

"Well, all right, then." Emma was suddenly anxious for him to leave, her offer to cook hanging in the air like an unwelcome sexual advance. "I think I can take it from here, if you want to get going."

He flicked a look at his watch. "Not want to, but need to." He took his wallet out of his back pocket and opened it, taking out three fifties and handing them to her. "This is your rate, isn't it?"

Emma found taking the money the hardest part of the job, and fought to keep a professional smile on her face. She wanted the money. She needed the money. She didn't know what it was inside her that didn't want to take cash directly from someone's hand.

Undoubtedly it was more of that pride that her grandmother had scolded her for.

"Thanks," she said stiffly, stuffing the bills in her back pocket. "You can leave it on the kitchen counter for me in the future. Here's my contact info," she said, handing him a business card printed off her computer. "I can send you a weekly or monthly invoice if you'd prefer."

He raised a brow. "Invoices are paper trails. You report all your income to the IRS?"

"Yes." She shrugged. "My friends say I shouldn't, that it would make financial sense to cheat a little, and I'd never be caught, but . . ."

He cocked his head slightly, looking at her. "But you aren't going to sell your soul for a couple bucks."

She smiled. "I'd prefer it to go for a much higher price."

"Like what?"

Like a toehold at a top architecture firm, if someone dangled such a temptation before her. "I haven't yet heard an offer that would tempt me." Her gaze unexpectedly locked with his. Silence pulled between them, and Emma felt a sudden panic thumping at her heart.

"Well, I—" He stepped back.

"You've got—" she said at the same time, the both of them speaking over each other, "—to get going," Emma finished.

"Yes." He pulled a card out of his own wallet and gave it to her. "My cell number is on here. Call me if you have any questions."

"Okay. Thanks."

"It was good to meet you," he said, holding out his hand. "I hope this works out well for us both."

"Yes, me too," Emma said, gingerly taking his hand. She felt the slight roughness of his palm slide along her own. His hand closed around hers and an image came to mind of him cupping his hand someplace much lower and more intimate. Liquid warmth ran through her thighs and her inner muscles clenched, her eyes slowly closing.

Oh, Lord. He'd better leave before she pushed down her jeans and demanded that he *take her, now!*

Then his hand released hers and he moved away, heading toward the kitchen and the door to the garage. Emma went back out the front door to fetch her things and to watch as the garage door rose and his black car silently pulled out, no sound of a motor detectable.

A hybrid. He drove an electric hybrid. Not just any hybrid, though: it was a Lexus GS 450h, and a pretty penny it must have cost. It was a fitting, eco-chic choice for a software millionaire in the Pacific Northwest, this most environmentally aware of regions.

Russ Carrick must want to attract women who knew which plastics could be put in the recycling bin. Or maybe he didn't give a soybean curd for what other people thought. She'd bet on the latter.

Emma waved good-bye, and a shadowy movement suggested he might be waving back. Then he was gone and she was alone with his empty, unlived-in house and her cleaning supplies.

Two

"They've moved the conference call to two o'clock this afternoon," Kevin said as Russ came in.

"Did they give a reason?"

Kevin shrugged. "They said they weren't ready, and one of the VPs had a family emergency and wasn't in yet."

Russ sighed and headed for his glass-walled office. The floor-to-ceiling windows looked out on the ship canal that joined Elliot Bay to Lake Union and Lake Washington. Programmers on the other side of the building had views of the side streets of the Fremont neighborhood of Seattle, a once-funky area that was quickly becoming trendy. The yearly solstice parade with its naked bicyclists still pedaled on, but the neighborhood didn't have the comfortable eccentricity it had before the overpriced clothing boutiques and upscale coffee shops and bistros had moved in.

He often felt like the same thing was happening to himself and the company he and his brother, James, had started together. Once freewheeling and creative, they had struggled to stay in the software race and build a company of their own, where they would be no one's employee. They'd started an online used bookstore and developed software to inventory and link used bookstores across the country. The bookstore had failed, but the software they created for it had been the genesis of TrackingTech, the company that now specialized in software for inventory tracking and distribution.

Their struggle had brought them to where Russ was now: primary shareholder and chief executive officer of a profitable company that was set to make an exponential leap in growth. Innovative programming was left to others, while Russ evolved into a businessman courting the favor of pharmaceutical companies, discount retailers, and grocery stores.

He and his brother had been as successful as they'd ever wished—and then nine months ago James had been killed at the age of thirty-eight. A drunk driver crossing the center line of traffic had hit James's car head-on. Russ, his sister, Pamela, their parents and their extended family, and James's legions of friends had had their hearts ripped out.

Pamela had reacted by becoming overprotective of her one remaining sibling. Thus her hiring of Emma for him, even though he didn't need a housekeeper. He'd only agreed because he understood how badly Pam needed to take care of him—as if having a spotless kitchen and ironed sheets could keep him from meeting an untimely end.

For Russ, the zest had gone out of life. He pursued business with automated determination, knowing that it couldn't fill the space left by James and yet not knowing what else to do. There were long afternoons when he stared out the office window at the boats passing through the canal and felt a longing for the early days with James, when he and his brother had both been naked solstice bike riders, if only metaphorically. The days when there had been nothing between them and a crash to the asphalt, but they knew they could rely on each other. There had been the sweet rush of cool freedom against their skin and a sense of endless possibility in the road ahead.

Now the future was blank, its shapes and possibilities lost or unknown. It was the undrawn portion of the map where the monsters lurked, and he had lost his navigator.

Kevin popped his head in the open doorway. "Hey, can I have your housekeeper's phone number?"

"You want someone to clean your house?"

"I want to ask her out." Kevin entered the office. "Do you think she'd say yes? She implied I'm not a bad catch."

"I don't want you dating my housekeeper." It was a knee-jerk reaction, something inside him rejecting the notion of Kevin laying his hands on Emma Mayson.

"Why not?"

Russ tried to think of a rational reason. "She's going to be going through my private stuff," he said, making it up as he went along. "It's not as if she signed a confidentiality agreement."

"You're afraid she'll spill secrets about you? Like what, that you leave towels on the bathroom floor? You don't have any secrets. Come on, give me her number."

"I'd rather you didn't get involved with her."

Kevin stared at him, and then his eyes widened. "Oh ho ho! You want her yourself!"

Russ scowled. "No, I don't."

"I don't blame you: she's hot. And bubbly. Who'd pass up hot and bubbly?"

"She's not a meat pie. And *I* would pass her up. Did you see that car of hers?" Russ said, trying to scare Kevin off. "Are you sure you could handle a woman who drove a car built for street racing? She's probably got bigger balls than either of us. Not exactly the take-home-to-Mama type."

A flicker of doubt passed over Kevin's face. "She seemed nice."

"She probably has a boyfriend in prison and three kids at home."

Kevin stared at him; then his natural ebullience resurfaced. "Yeah, right! Just give me her number and I'll ask her."

"Kevin. She's my employee, and she must be ten years younger than either of us. Leave her alone."

"I wouldn't mind playing sugar daddy."

Russ laughed. "I can't quite see you in that role."

"I can be a jerk if I try hard enough. And I'm sick of losing women to assholes."

Well, hell, Kevin would have better luck if he stopped getting involved with women recovering from breakups with assholes. They used his kind-hearted friend for sympathy and confidence-building; then when they felt strong again they went back to the jerks.

Maybe someone as seemingly normal as Emma would be good for Kevin, despite Russ's gut rejection of the idea. "I wouldn't feel right giving out Emma's number without her permission. I'll ask her if I can give it to you. How's that?"

"As good as I'll get, apparently. You'll ask her today?"

Russ raised an exasperated brow. "Don't push me."

"Just didn't want you waiting until next year. The sooner you do it, the sooner I'll stop asking you about it."

"Tell me again why I keep you working for me."

"Because I'm the only one not afraid of your sour temper."

"Get out of here," Russ said without heat.

" '*Emma, my lovely Emma . . .*' " Kevin sang as he left the room.

His sour temper. Russ grimaced. Was that how people saw him now, as a grouch?

Was that what Emma Mayson had seen? He mentally reviewed their tour through the house, remembering how brusquely he had answered her small-talk remarks. She'd been lobbing him conversational softballs and he'd swatted

21

them to the ground one after the other until she gave up. She'd probably thought him a grumpy tight-ass, instead of what he really was: a geeky guy who'd never learned to relax around an attractive woman.

Emma Mayson was young and beautiful and socially at ease, and completely out of his range. She probably went to nightclubs and . . . and . . . whatever people her age and type did with their free time. He'd never moved in socially active crowds. Social activists, yes. But no dance-till-dawn club hoppers. Emma and he probably didn't have a thing in common.

He pulled her business card out of his wallet, absently running his finger up and down the edge. He could call her right now and pass on Kevin's request.

The imaginary conversation flowed through his head. Him, awkward and embarrassed to be playing high school go-between. Her, uncomfortable being put on the spot, forced to decide whether or not to reject a man she'd met for only a moment, and not sure if her decision would impact her job at Russ's house.

He tossed the card on his desk; he couldn't think about it now.

He spun around to stare out the windows. Instead of passing motorboats, however, it was Emma Mayson he saw, pulling the sheets off his bed and examining them for signs of "activities."

Yikes! Appeasing his sister was one thing. Beautiful

young women washing his underwear was another. He had to put an end to it right now.

He reached for the phone and quickly dialed Emma's cell number, hoping she'd pick up before he could think twice, since the second thoughts were already creeping in—Pamela's disappointed face gazing sad-eyed at him. On the fifth ring, Emma's breathless voice answered.

"Hello?"

"Emma? This is Russ Carrick."

"Oh, hi! I was wondering who it could be. The caller ID said 'TrackingTech.' "

"Yes, that's my company."

"What do you track? Stolen cars? Wild animals with radio collars?"

"Nothing so exciting. We design software for tracking inventory."

"Oh."

Oh, she'd said. *Oh, how boring.* "You'd be surprised how big an industry it is. Everything from apples to the chemicals used in producing drugs has to be tracked by companies."

"Oh!" she said again, and he could hear her effort to sound fascinated.

He pressed the heel of his hand against his forehead, shutting his eyes against the embarrassment of trying to impress her with inventory software. "Yes, well, the reason I'm calling—"

"You're taking me up on my offer to cook for you?" she said, hope and excitement in her voice.

"No, I uh . . ." Christ, firing someone was always so hard.

"Oh." A world of disappointment in that one sound. She didn't say anything more, the soft crackling of the cell connection filling the space between them.

Ah, dammit. She probably needed this job. He sighed.

"Yes?" she said timidly.

He rubbed his face. It wouldn't kill him to let her clean his bathroom for a month or two—he'd just be sure to clean it himself, first, so there wasn't anything embarrassing for her to find. "I'm, er . . . calling about Kevin, the man you met at my house. The one with the Jaguar."

"Oh?"

He smiled. Who knew that one vowel sound could convey so many different things? "This is awkward. He asked for your phone number."

There was a short silence, and then she said warily, "I'm assuming by your tone that he didn't want it in order to hire me."

"No."

"Ah."

"How about I give you his number, and you can call or not as you please? There's no need for you to give me any sort of answer."

"No, let's not do that," she said.

Conflicting emotions tumbled through his chest. Glee

that she would not be dating Kevin, and embarrassment and a twinge of pain on Kevin's behalf.

Her tone turned brisk. "If he wants to ask me out, he should do it himself. None of this junior high 'he said, she said' nonsense, and *I'm* certainly not going to call *him* for a date. Go ahead and give him my number."

A shot of disappointment went through him, along with envy that Kevin had had the nerve to make an overture toward her. Russ would never have guessed that she would find Kevin attractive; that he would be her type. "So you're going to say yes?"

She was quiet for a long moment. "I don't know. What would you do?"

"If Kevin asked me out?"

She laughed. "You know the guy. Is he a good person? Does he treat people well?"

"I've no doubt he'll make an excellent husband. For the right woman," he qualified.

"No telling whether that's me, though, is there? But I'm not looking for a husband at this point in my life," she went on. "Is he looking for a wife?"

"I'd have to let him answer that."

"But your impression?"

"My impression is yes, he's ready to settle down and start a family."

He heard the breath of a sigh at the other end. "I'm twenty-six," she said. "How old is Kevin?"

"Kevin's thirty-three."

"And you?"

"I'm a little older."

"Thirty-four, thirty-five, forty?"

He grimaced. "Thirty-six."

She laughed. "Yeah, you're positively decrepit."

"Maybe this isn't a good idea, your going out with Kevin," he said. Somehow it was easier to talk to her when he couldn't see her; when her lively eyes weren't upon him and he wasn't distracted by the silky locks of her ponytail hanging over her shoulder and down over the curve of her breast. Or by the way her low-cut jeans molded to her pert backside, as if inviting a man to put his hands on either side of her hips and pull her back against him.

"No, let him call me," she said. "You never know, we might hit it off. Maybe something unexpectedly good will come from it."

His heart sank. "Expecting the worst and hoping for the best?"

"It seems a reasonable approach to life." She laughed. "But it usually turns out to be neither the best nor the worst, does it?"

"How so?"

"It usually turns out to be Option C, the outcome you never considered. The one you never saw coming."

His own laugh was tinged with sorrow. "That's more true than I'd like to admit."

"Eh," she said, a shrug in her voice. "It keeps things interesting."

When the call was over he stared out his windows for a long time, watching the boats and thinking about Emma Mayson and her blithe spirit.

James would have liked her. She was a solstice bike rider, untouched as yet by the asphalt of life.

He hoped she stayed that way forever.

Three

Emma shut her cell phone off, glared at it, then turned it back on again, threw it on her bed, and blew out a breath of exasperation.

Why, oh why, had she said that Russ's friend could call her?

The prospect of turning Kevin down made her sweat each time the phone rang. Rejection was crushing on the receiving end, but it was little better for the one who rejected.

Would she have been so quick to reject Kevin if she hadn't seen him standing next to Russell Carrick, looking like a poor shadow? Looking smaller, clumsier, less confident, like an adolescent instead of a fully grown man?

Or maybe she would have thought Kevin a potential boyfriend if she hadn't spent five minutes talking to Russ on the phone, enjoying the sound of his deep voice. If she hadn't heard him be more expansive than on the stiff tour of his house. If he hadn't sounded a little sad, hadn't shown a hint of humor, hadn't so obviously been trying to protect both Kevin's and her feelings.

Ah Foolishness, thy name is Woman. Witness her initial thought that Russ had called to ask her out.

And foolish she still was, because what had she been doing all evening except looking up Russ Carrick on the Internet?

She almost wished she hadn't. It wasn't as much fun to fantasize about a man who was the primary shareholder of a company listed on the NASDAQ at $150 a share. It put him at a far different stage in his life than she was; far different than she'd *ever* be. She didn't want to ride on a man's coattails of financial success, or to feel inferior to him based on her earnings.

And then there'd been the article about his brother's death. She knew something of bereavement from her childhood, when her father had died of a heart attack, and from her teen years, when her grandmother had died. Memories of those feelings didn't give her any clue of what to say to someone else experiencing grief, though: all she knew was that there *were* no words of comfort.

She didn't know how to relate to a man like Russ Carrick. She didn't know how to read him. Didn't know how to anticipate his reactions like she would with a gooberish boy her own age.

Still, he had a nice ass. And she liked his voice. His eyes. The width of his shoulders . . .

God, she'd love to have him pin her naked beneath him and—

"Hey, Ems, whatcha doing?" her roommate, Daphne, said, sticking her head inside Emma's open doorway.

"Nothing! Just thinking."

Daphne came in and sat on the edge of the bed. Her highlighted blond hair looked freshly flatironed and sprayed, her eye makeup set to "evening." She was wearing a turquoise silk halter top and gold hoop earrings. "You're always thinking. Give it a rest, and come out with me and Derek."

Emma grimaced. "And be the third wheel? No thanks."

"We're meeting Josie and Ken at the Palomino bar, then going dancing. Come on, you might have fun!"

"I'd really rather not. I want to keep studying the building codes." She patted the fat binder on her desk.

Daphne blew a raspberry. "You *never* go out. How are you going to meet someone if you never go out?"

"I don't want to meet someone right now. I've got other things to worry about, like finding a real job."

Daphne rolled her eyes. "You're not going to miss out on a job opportunity by going out for one night."

"It's just not my cup of tea."

She shrugged and got up. "Have it your way. But socializing is good for job seekers, you know. Friends hooking you up with friends of friends who know the right people."

"I'd love to schmooze my way into a job, but I'm no good

at schmoozing, so why try? I have more faith in presenting a solid knowledge of building codes."

"You don't give yourself enough credit. My friends all think you're charming. You could schmooze with the best."

Emma perked up. "Who thinks I'm charming?"

"All of them! And they don't understand why you stay home every night."

Emma gave her a suspicious look. "I seriously doubt they spare a moment's thought for me."

Daphne grinned. "Some of the guys do, believe me."

"Mmm." Emma tried to sound uncaring but she was flattered, and it prompted her to share, "Someone asked for my number today."

Daphne plopped back down on the bed. "Yeah? Who?"

Emma shrugged. "An older guy, kind of geeky."

Daphne wrinkled her nose. "Oh. Are you going to go out with him?"

"I don't know."

"What type of car does he drive?"

Emma laughed. "A new Jaguar. He'd be glad to know you asked."

"It's a valid question! You can tell a lot about a person by their car."

"Can you?" she said, thinking of Russ's hybrid.

"Well, not about *you*," Daphne said, waving away the comment. "A case of false advertising, there."

Emma had bought her souped-up Honda from her

brother, whose pregnant wife had demanded that the street racer be put out to pasture. It was a difficult and ornery car, with stiff shocks, a primer-coated hood and fender, and a frightening red button on the shift for setting off the nitrous system power booster. Emma expected that someday the car would run off with her like a spooked racehorse.

Daphne added, "But I've always wondered if there's a secret wild side to you."

"I doubt it," Emma said, with less than the ring of truth. She was too sensible to act on the impulses for spontaneous lunacy that sometimes swept over her.

Daphne nodded knowingly, eyes narrowing. "I think there is. And someday it's going to spring out and scare the living shit out of you."

"Maybe when I'm eighty-five and senile."

Daphne stood and headed from the room, pausing at the door to smile back at her. "Don't make it wait that long. You're only young once. Use that body while you have it!"

Emma brooded on that parting remark for the next hour and a half, thinking about her sexual dry spell. Common sense and caution did have a way of taking the fun out of life.

Or maybe it wasn't caution that held her back from bursts of ecstatic lunacy, but caution's evil twin: cowardice. That worry had haunted her since one of her professors, an architect whose skills and talent she deeply respected, had commented that her designs were "safe." Adequate and buildable, unlike some of her classmates' impractical designs, yet there was little about her work that would inspire anyone to build it. But there were small flashes of creative genius, he'd told her. Here and there, in the treatment of a staircase or a roofline, he saw a glimmer of what she was capable of.

He had given her a B minus and told her that she'd be stuck doing architectural grunt work her whole career unless she learned to open up to her creative side, to stop being afraid of her own ideas.

She supposed he'd intended the comment to wake her up and inspire her, but all it had done was undercut her confidence, not knowing how to make herself more courageously creative. She'd thought she *was* being creative, and didn't know where this hidden genius was supposed to be residing or how to force it out of its hidey-hole.

The phone rang, jolting her out of her dark thoughts. She lunged for it, then held it in her hand without answering, dreading the conversation to come.

She swallowed her cowardice and flipped open the phone. "Hello?"

"Emma?" a male voice asked, voice cracking in the middle of her name.

"Yes?"

Throat clearing. " 'Scuse me. This is Kevin," he went on, voice warbling somewhere around normality. "We met today at Russ's house?"

"Yes, hello. He told me that you might be calling."

"And here I am!" He laughed and then coughed.

Her last bits of hope for a potential match were fading fast. A silence stretched between them, in which she could almost hear the nervous tension thrumming through his wiry body. "How's your car?" she asked, for lack of anything better to say. "Get any scratches or dings this afternoon?"

"A rock chip in my windshield as I was driving home. Can you believe it!"

"Ooh, bad luck, there. I hope it won't be too expensive to fix."

He took the topic and ran with it for the next five minutes, apparently taking Emma's *mmms* and *ahs* and polite questions as signs of interest. Her mind began to wander to one of her favorite mental escapes: designing her dream bathroom. *What were the codes for placement of electrical outlets near water, again?* She eyed the binder, her fingers itching to flip it open and check.

"So I was thinking," Kevin said, "maybe you'd like to go for a drive out to Snoqualmie Falls, and we can have dinner at the lodge there."

"Dinner?" she said, snapping back to the present, a wall of cobalt blue glass tiles fading from her vision.

"I thought it would be a pretty drive."

"I'm sure it would be—"

"Great! How about Friday?"

She hadn't meant to say *yes*; she hadn't meant to imply

an answer one way or the other! "This week isn't good," she fibbed.

"The Friday after, then. Or the Saturday—we could make a day of it! Maybe drive all the way to Ellensburg—"

"No!" Emma interrupted in a panic. "No, no, dinner would be better."

"Okay," he said, sounding disappointed.

"Friday after next, dinner, Snoqualmie Falls," Emma repeated, trying to sound cheerful and wondering how she'd managed to get locked into a date she didn't want. Too late to back out now, though.

Kevin quickly wrapped up the call, seeming to sense his perilous hold on her, and Emma snapped her phone shut. "Well, that sucks," she said aloud, and went out to the kitchen to get a bowl of ice cream.

Daphne had left a newspaper on the table, and Emma sat down with her ice cream and unfolded the front section. She skimmed the headlines and her gaze caught on the one at the bottom of the page:

King Street Station on Track for Design Contest

She dropped her spoon back into her bowl, her eyes eagerly taking in the details of the article.

The City of Seattle, the Burlington Northern Santa Fe freight company that owned the tracks, the federal government, and private investors were coming together to fund a complete teardown and reconstruction of the King Street train station. The new design would be decided by a panel of judges, chosen from the pool of entries in a contest. The winning designer or design team would be offered a contract to work on the new station.

The King Street Station was the only train station in Seattle, there being no subway. Emma had been to it once or twice to pick up friends who had taken Amtrak, and the place was a dump. Not only was it in serious disrepair, with plywood nailed over crumbling walls and two-thirds of the building off limits to all but the rats, but the only access was from a dead-end street with nowhere to turn around, making for chaos between taxis, buses, and hapless passenger cars all trying to get in and out.

Emma abandoned her ice cream and dashed back to her room with newspaper in hand, her heart thumping with excitement. At her computer, she typed in the URL to the website with the contest details. Professors in grad school had frequently used design contests from all over the country as assignments, but none of her work had ever been judged good enough by a professor to be sent in.

But that didn't mean she couldn't succeed this time, in her own city. She understood Seattle and its zeitgeist; she could create something that spoke to its people. She could *do* this!

The contest site said that preliminary judging would be of a two-dimensional poster board. Ten finalists would present their ideas in front of the judges, the press, the project backers, and any of the interested public.

If she could make it to the finals, it might be the break she'd been looking for. Big professional design teams would surely be entering. Being a finalist alongside them would be a fabulous opportunity to network and schmooze! And if nothing else, it would be a big fat star on her résumé.

This could be it. If she really set herself free, if she really dug down and unearthed that inner creative genius, maybe things would finally take a turn for the better. Maya Lin, the woman who won the contest to design the Vietnam Veterans Memorial, had also been graded average by her professors, and now her name was one of the few that Joe Public recognized in contemporary architecture.

What worked for Maya Lin might work for Emma Mayson, too.

Four

Russ turned on the shower and tilted the nozzle so it hit the tiles he'd just scrubbed, rinsing away the cleanser. He cursed as water dripped down his arm and into the sleeve of his shirt.

This was ridiculous. He'd spent the last two hours cleaning his house in preparation for Emma's arrival *to clean his house.* He'd only meant to clean up any embarrassing bits of personal dirt, but suddenly it had seemed that such bits were everywhere. He didn't want her finding a stray toenail clipping on the carpet or a body hair on a sheet; didn't want her finding gunk around his shower drain or a crusty dish on the counter, or coffee grounds under the sink where they'd missed the trash can. The thought of her cleaning up after him *bothered* him.

If she were older, or married, or unattractive either physically or emotionally, then he wouldn't care. But she was none of those things. She was *hot*.

A guy doesn't want a hot girl scrubbing his toilet and muttering to herself what a filthy pig he is. Even if the guy didn't have a chance in hell with her, even if one of his friends has managed to get a *date* with her—a friggin' date!—he still doesn't want that.

He shut off the shower and perked his ears at a distant sound. Did he hear something? She wasn't here already, was she? He cursed again and went to check on his laundry, anxious to get the next load into the wash and safely out of her reach. He could not have her touching his Jockeys; he just couldn't.

He also couldn't go through this frantic cleaning every Wednesday, in anticipation of her arrival.

As he loaded his hockey Puck Skins and other darks into the dryer, he imagined what his brother, James, would have said about all this. "Jump her, you idiot! Or at least make a move on her. Kevin has a date, not a legal claim. Since you don't want her cleaning your house anyway, what have you got to lose?"

James had been a bit of a cad with women, but always managed to find plenty who were willing to put up with his shenanigans. James said they had their eyes on the prize: marriage in a community property state.

Russ had his doubts. Despite his joking comments to

Kevin about gold diggers, his impression was that women had better ways to earn money these days than marry for it. He hadn't met many who were willing to put up with an asshole for the sake of a bigger house.

No, women had put up with James because he was fun and clearly loved them. To James, all women were beautiful and witty and worthy of attention. He would have made a pass at Emma within five seconds of meeting her, and would have done so in a light, flirtatious manner that would make her smile even if she wasn't interested.

His ear caught the distant sound of a female voice, talking as if on a cell phone. She *was* here.

And he didn't have either James's talent for seduction or his willingness to compete with a friend for a woman's affections.

Damn.

He got the next load of laundry running and went to find Emma to say hello. The talking had stopped and the house was silent as he walked through it. He saw her cleaning supplies in the foyer but no Emma.

Where was she?

He was making his second round of the house when a small sound directed his attention to his recliner in the great room. She was flopped in it, staring blankly out the window, her cell phone lying in her hand.

She looked on the verge of tears. As he watched, her mouth turned down at a painful angle, eyes squeezing shut, face reddening as tears rolled out her lids and down her cheeks. Her lips parted and a soft wheeze of pain whistled out.

Ah, hell! Now what was he supposed to do? He looked frantically around for a Kleenex or an escape route. She couldn't want him to see this. God knew *he* didn't want to see this.

Before he could make a move either way, her eyes opened and she saw him. He froze like an animal in a hunter's spotlight. Her eyes widened, and then the crying seemed to take on a new, more violent force.

"Great! Oh, just great!" she said, wiping her face with her bare hands as her tears and nose ran freely. "This just tops it." She dropped her hands to glare at him. "What are you *doing* here? Aren't you supposed to be at work?"

"I, uh . . . Excuse me!" He bolted for the kitchen, grabbed a clean dish towel, then jogged back to her holding it out. "Here."

She snorted noisily and reached for it. "Thanks," she mumbled, and wiped at her face. She dabbed discreetly at her nose, then looked up at him over the red and blue cloth, red-rimmed eyes tinged with accusation.

Was she expecting something more from him? *What,* for God's sake? He scrambled back through memory to his last serious relationship, in which he'd had to deal with frequent female tears. With great reluctance he offered, "Do you, er . . . need a hug?"

She dropped the cloth from her face and scowled. "No!" Then her lips started to quiver, the sides dipping downward again.

Oh God.

He gritted his teeth and inched toward her, arms open, hoping she wouldn't hurt him. Emotional women were like grumpy bears, in his experience. They were ready to disembowel you at the first wrong move.

She jumped up out of the chair and batted his arm away. "I said I don't need a hug! I'm just having a very bad day."

"Okaaay." Easy there, she-bear. If he could back away quietly . . .

She glared at him, looked away, then flew at him in a sudden rush. He stepped back in alarm, but not quickly enough to keep her from attaching herself to his chest in a hug, arms going around his rib cage and squeezing the breath out of him as she burrowed her face into his shirt.

When his mind cleared of its adrenaline fog, he remembered to put his arms around her. He patted her back as she sobbed and shook, then as she started to settle down, he changed to a gentle rub. He felt the band of her bra beneath her tight T-shirt, and the soft firmness of warm skin over muscle and bone. He became aware of her breasts pressed against his chest.

Her breathing eased and her grip loosened as she relaxed against him. "That feels nice," she said softly.

Her whispered words went straight from his ear down to

his groin, stirring an erection to life. He gently disentangled himself and stepped back. "Are you okay now?"

Her eyes were puffy, but she managed a rueful smile. "Yeah. Sorry about that." She pulled out a chair from the big dining table and sat down. "It's been one of those days where things all pile up at once and something inside you just gives, you know?"

He pulled out another chair and sat, grateful for the chance to hide his arousal. He didn't want to hear a litany of woes, but neither did he want to be callous and leave her.

She shook her head. "It's all small stuff, in the scheme of things. I shouldn't have let it get to me." She smiled again. "Thanks for the hug, and for putting up with me. I'm okay now; you can go to work."

With the prospect of a litany of woes swept away from him, he was suddenly curious about what had set her off. "Something didn't happen to someone in your family, did it?" he asked.

"Oh, no! Nothing like that. No, it's all petty stuff, like I said. Someone broke a window out of my car last night and stole the radio. I got two rejection letters in the mail today from firms where I'd interviewed. My student loan, car insurance, health insurance, and quarterly taxes are all due, and my roommate just called and told me that she's moving in with her boyfriend next week, which means my rent just doubled." She laughed, but it sounded tinged with hysteria. "That's all. Nothing serious!"

"No, nothing serious, but I remember those days myself. Everything hung together as long as nothing went wrong, but when something did go wrong, I was screwed."

She looked at him with interest. "Yeah? What did you do when that happened?"

"Slept on friends' couches and only ate the free food at the pizza place where I worked. That was while I was in college."

Her mouth quirked. "I suppose I could live in my car and eat out of the refrigerators at the houses where I clean."

"I doubt it will come to that. Do you want some coffee?" His arousal had gone down, and he felt safe standing.

"Sure."

Emma followed him into the kitchen, bemused by the turn the day had taken. With each sucky thing that happened, she had felt herself sinking lower and lower under the weight of her situation. It hadn't helped that she had PMS, had stayed up until four in the morning working out and rejecting ideas for the train station, and all she'd eaten today was a banana.

Still, she'd thought she was holding up all right through car break-in, rejection letters, and bills until Daphne called, ecstatic over Derek's proposal that she move in with him. The moment Emma hung up, emotion had washed over her, unstoppable as the tide.

The last thing she'd expected was that Russ would witness her meltdown. The poor man had looked as horrified as she was.

She bit her lip against a smile, thinking of his offer of a hug. He'd dealt with her emotions the best he could. He had no idea that taking him up on his offer had more to do with the chance to touch him than it did with her need for solace. Yet something about the simple physical contact had soothed her, and once her nose cleared she realized that she liked how he smelled. She'd have happily stayed in his embrace all day.

She took a seat on one of the tall stools at the kitchen island while Russ set about making coffee.

"There are times I'm almost nostalgic for that time of my life," he said.

"I'll trade you."

He shook his head. "I wouldn't take the memories from you. It makes success all the sweeter."

She put her elbows on the counter and rested her chin in her palms. "Success. I begin to wonder if I'll ever find it."

"What type of firms did you interview at?"

"I have a master's degree in architecture. I'm trying to find an internship position."

He stared at her. "A master's degree?"

"So you wonder why I'm cleaning houses, don't you?"

"Yes. In a word."

"It was supposed to be temporary." She held up her fingers, counting off: "The money is okay, it takes no training, you don't have to give notice when you quit, I get to see inside a lot of houses and see both bad and good design, I can arrange my schedule to allow for interviews, and the work doesn't take any brain power, so I can save my thinking energy for things I care about."

She dropped her chin back into her hands. "Only the money turns out to be not quite good enough to cover a perfect storm of bills and circumstance."

"Why not take a regular job, if that's what it takes to make ends meet?"

"I'm afraid of getting sidetracked. I'm afraid I'll get lost in some other career, and architecture will become the thing I always wanted to do but didn't. And by the time I try to go back to it, it'll be too late. All my knowledge will be out of date and my ideas won't have evolved with the times. I won't be a wannabe anymore; I'll be a wanted-to-be."

"So what are you going to do?" he asked, setting a mug of coffee in front of her. "Cream, sugar?"

"Both, thanks." She stirred her coffee and noticed him giving the same treatment to his own coffee. Heavy on the cream, heavy on the sugar, like a mug of hot coffee ice cream. "I don't know what I'm going to do. Try to get more work, I suppose." She sipped her coffee, thinking about Daphne moving in with Derek. Daphne said that Derek didn't want her to contribute toward his mortgage; that he wanted her there because he loved her, not because he wanted to save a few bucks.

"Do you know what I think sometimes?" Emma mused aloud.

He raised a brow. "No."

"I sometimes think that it would suit me perfectly fine to be a man's mistress."

His brows went up.

"I'm not the only woman to ever think it, you know," she said in mock-seriousness. "And I don't mean *mistress* in the sense of a married man's lover. I mean that sometimes it seems like it would be a pretty good deal to be a man's kept woman. Have him pay my living expenses in exchange for on-demand sex." She grinned. "Hey, I'm horny anyway. It would kill a couple birds with one stone."

"Could you *do* that? Emotionally?"

She shrugged, a half smile on her lips. He didn't think she was serious, did he? "Who knows? Maybe. If the situation was right."

Could she really do it? Probably not. Not unless it was someone like Russ, whom she wanted to sleep with anyway. She made a show of tapping her fingertips along her jaw and tilted her head, looking up at the ceiling as if considering. "I'd have to like the guy, or at least respect him. And I'd have to find him physically attractive." She slid a glance toward him and smiled wickedly.

He looked stunned. "I thought women wanted love with sex. Marriage. Children."

She dropped her hands to the counter. "Oh, I do, but in a few years. Right now, I don't want my life to get swallowed up in a romantic relationship."

"Swallowed up?"

"I don't want my ambition to get diluted by attachment to a guy. I've got too much to do, too much to achieve, before I get wrapped up in a relationship."

The look on his face was one of utter befuddlement. "I don't think I've ever met a woman who felt the way you do about love and sex."

She waved her hand dismissively. "Don't take me seriously. The mistress stuff was just an idle thought. Surely you've had impractical fantasies too?"

He laughed. "You just described the perfect fantasy of a lot of men. A beautiful young woman who wants regular sex from him but no emotional entanglements."

She chuckled, feeling a bit better. "Well, there you go. And speaking of going, don't you have to go to work?"

"I have some things to do in my home office; then I'll go in."

She slid off the bar stool. "Well, thanks for the coffee and sympathy. I have another house to do after yours, so I'd better get cracking."

She was happy for an excuse to get away from him. *God.* What was wrong with her?

You want to get into his pants, that's what's wrong, her inner voice said as she went to fetch her vacuum. She'd noticed in the past that when talking to an attractive guy, she gave away her interest by turning the conversation to sex. Never in an, "Oh baby, take me home tonight" way; she talked about sex under the guise of having a pseudo-intellectual discussion. She'd mention a *Cosmo* poll or a factoid heard on TV related to sex, and ask his opinion. The words would spill out of her mouth before she consciously knew she liked a guy.

She shut her eyes, shaking her head in embarrassment. She'd outdone herself this time. She'd all but offered to be Russ's paid love slave. What must he think of her?

"*Criminy*," she said under her breath, borrowing a word from her deceased grandmother. The day just couldn't get any worse.

Russ answered e-mails in his home office, clearing the most pressing out of his in-box.

The distraction worked for a while, but then he heard Emma vacuuming the hall outside the office, working her way through the house toward his bedroom. He felt for her, trying to find her footing in the world, and wished he could help. Unfortunately, he didn't know any architects who he might ask to give her special consideration.

However, he did own an apartment downtown that he could rent to her for a pittance until she got back on her feet. He himself may have slept on the borrowed couches of friends, but he didn't like to think of a young woman doing that. Bad things could happen: a friend's boyfriend, drunk, finding Emma asleep and vulnerable and taking advantage of the opportunity. A single woman needed to keep herself out of danger.

His old apartment had been sitting empty for the three months since the last tenant moved out. He'd been meaning to put it on the market but hadn't gotten around to it.

He smiled. It was gratifying to have procrastination turn out to be fortuitous.

He could also hire her to cook and grocery shop, as she'd offered last week. He was sick of restaurant food and frozen dinners; it would be nice to have real meals at home. At least until she got on her feet. Sooner or later she'd land the internship position she was looking for, and she'd drop the cooking and cleaning in an instant.

He imagined the the smile, the relief on her face when he made the offers.

Then he frowned.

She *would* be relieved, wouldn't she? Or would she be offended? She might think he thought she couldn't take care of herself, that he thought her a charity case. She might see him as overprotective, trying to take away her independence.

Dammit, why wasn't anything ever easy?

Emma rapped on the door frame and stuck her head in. "Hi. I think I'm done, unless you want me to clean in here?"

"No, I'd never find anything again. You're done already?" Crap! He hadn't had time to think out how to make his offer.

Emma took a step into the office. "Yeah, the place is spotless. But it was nearly spotless before I got here. Are you always so neat, or did you clean before I arrived?"

At the look of guilt on his face, Emma bit the inside of her lip, trying not to giggle. "I've seen boy mess before, you know. I have a brother."

He scrubbed his hand through his hair and sighed. "Do you have a minute?"

"Sure." She stepped closer and leaned against the leather visitor chair in front of his desk. "What's up?"

He looked at her and then away, his jaw hard. "This is uncomfortable," he muttered.

The thought fluttered through her mind that he was going to fire her. *Oh God, no, not today of all days! I shouldn't have broken down; I shouldn't have said all those stupid things!* He wouldn't be so heartless, would he, when he knew what a difficult position she was in?

He gestured toward the chair. "Sit. Please."

She slid over the arm and into place, hands in her lap like a good girl, afraid to say anything.

"I don't want to offend you, Emma, so please don't take this the wrong way. It's not a comment on your character."

Oh God, oh God, oh God . . .

"I have an apartment downtown, in the Belltown neighborhood. It's been empty for three months. I was thinking that you could stay there. And that I would take you up on your offer."

It took several seconds for her brain to make sense of his words. As they sank in, her heart seemed to stop. *He wanted her to be his mistress?*

51

"I don't want you to think this is out of pity, or that I don't respect your independence."

Her heart lurched into motion again. *He was serious! Oh God, he was serious. What was she supposed to say?*

"You're not offended, are you?" he asked warily.

She blinked. "No, I don't think so. I mean, I offered, right? And it would obviously help me out. A lot." She chewed her lip. "*If* I said yes, how often would you want . . ." She trailed off, finishing the question with her eyebrows.

"I don't think I need it every night. Maybe, oh, Monday, Wednesday, Friday? With something big on Friday to last me through the weekend? You'd have the weekends off, of course."

"Of course!" Was she really having this discussion? "Er, what type of 'big' did you mean, for Fridays?"

He shrugged. "Big. You know, lots of it. I'll leave the details up to you."

"Ah. Are there any particular, um . . . *flavors* that you prefer? It might help me to have a starting point."

"I'm happy with most anything, so feel free to use your imagination." He smiled, meeting her eyes. "It sounds like you're willing?"

His warm gaze went straight to her loins, despite his insane proposition. She never would have guessed he would be up for such an arrangement. Never! Yet he'd said himself that she'd described the perfect male fantasy.

She could stand up and slap him, then storm out of his

house. But it wasn't what she wanted to do. What she wanted—against all common sense—was to say yes.

"I need to think about this," she said instead and shifted in her chair, distressingly aware of the arousal pooling down low, imagining him doing wicked things to her body three times a week.

"The choices will be all mine?" she asked, for clarification. "You'll take what I give you?"

"If that's the way you want it, although I'd appreciate it if you'd consider requests."

"Of course I would. I'd want you to be happy, after all. Isn't that the point?"

"I'd like you to enjoy it, too," he said. "I shouldn't like it to be a dreary chore for you. So be creative. Explore. Try new things. I'm up for it."

"Apparently so." She smiled, but he didn't appear to get the joke.

"You're proving very difficult to hire for a position you suggested yourself," he said with a touch of impatience.

"What do you expect? I've never done it before! I mean I've *done* it, but never for money. Never like this."

"It will be awkward for us both at first, I imagine."

"Yeah, I think so," she said, relieved that he felt the same way.

"Just like it's awkward discussing payment."

"Very awkward. *Extremely* awkward."

"I can get a prepaid Visa card for you, so you can buy

what you need. I know there will be a lot of shopping involved. And then should I pay you by the hour? Or would you prefer a set rate per night?"

Emma swallowed. How much did call girls make? A couple hundred a visit, at least. But if she was already getting her rent free and he was giving her spending money, that was worth a lot right there. And she wasn't going to be a call girl. Being a mistress was different—wasn't it?

"How about we do it by month?" She gathered her courage. "A thousand dollars."

He blew out a breath and leaned back in his chair. "*Hoo.* Steep."

"It's probably less than the going rate."

"You think so?"

"Yeah, I do."

He grimaced. "I don't know. It sounds like a lot."

She shrugged. "Take it or leave it: I'm not going to sell myself cheap. Besides, it's cheaper than a girlfriend, right? And not half so troublesome."

"Or I could do it myself."

"What fun is that? Besides, I don't see any signs that you've been satisfying your appetites." She leaned forward and lowered her voice. "I'd make it well worth it. I'd do my best to please you, however you want."

He cleared his throat. "You make it hard to refuse."

"Then don't. You'll enjoy it, I promise. And if you don't . . ." She shrugged and sat back. "We can always end the arrangement. Just promise not to make me move out of the apartment before I find someplace to go."

"No, of course not."

"And I probably shouldn't keep cleaning your house. That would be too weird, and you don't need a housekeeper anyway."

"I don't know about 'weird,' but it's true that I don't need someone to vacuum. I can do that myself."

"Then we have a deal?" Her heart fluttered, sensing that something momentous was about to happen in her life. Something insane and life-changing.

There was a long moment of silence, his thoughts unreadable on his face. And then: "What the hell. Let's do it!"

Oh boy. She smiled shakily. "How soon can I move into the apartment?"

"As soon as you like." He opened a drawer and took out a set of keys, then began scrawling information on a piece of notepaper. "Here's the address. There's parking under the building; the apartment has its own space. There's also a storage room in the basement. Will you need any help moving?"

"I have friends who can help."

He pushed the keys and piece of paper across the desk to her. "We can straighten out the utilities and the rest later. I know that moving is a lot of work, so I won't expect you to start your new duties for a week or two. When do think you'll be able to begin?"

She blinked. It was all so *businesslike*. "The Friday after this one?"

"Excellent! Could you have dinner ready by seven?"

He wanted her to cook for him, too? Apparently he was looking for one-stop shopping for all his appetites. That Visa card had better be loaded with plenty of cash if she had to buy groceries for romantic dinners. "You want the full deal, huh? Dinner *and* dessert?"

"Sure, if that's not too much for you. Given the price you asked, it seems a reasonable request."

"I can handle it, if that's really what you want." Damn. He was a sneaky negotiator, throwing that in at the last moment.

"It might be nice. Nothing too rich, though. I'm trying to eat right." He stood. "Okay, then."

She stood, too. "Okay, I guess." She turned and walked blindly to the door, but before she stepped through it a few crucial issues fought their way to the forefront of her stunned mind. She turned around.

"Two things."

"Yes?"

"One: you will get a complete physical and show me the paperwork saying that you're free of sexually transmitted diseases. I'll do the same for you. And two: this will be a monogamous relationship. I care about my health, just as I'm sure you care about yours."

He looked confused. "A physical? Why would that—" His

eyes widened as if in sudden understanding. "Oh. Oh, you think—"

She held up her hand. "As far as I know, I'm clear, and you may believe the same about yourself. But let's get the paperwork so neither of us has to worry about it. Sound reasonable?"

He nodded, his eyes still wide.

She felt better, seeing that he wasn't as in control as she'd thought. "Hey, relax! Remember, this was both our fantasies. If it doesn't work, at least we're giving it a shot. That's more than most people would dare."

"Much more," he said hoarsely.

"So, rah rah for courage and the unexpected!"

"Rah rah," he repeated faintly.

"Not something to put on my résumé, but maybe something to put in my memoirs, eh?"

"Emma, I—" he started, and then stopped, the words hanging there.

"You—?"

"I—I never expected something like this."

She wondered if that was what he had meant to say, but smiled. "Like I said before: it's the unexpected that keeps life interesting."

Five

Russ took a hit and landed flat on his back on the ice, staring up through his mask at the high ceiling of the Aurora Ice Arena. A moment later his teammate Greg appeared through his gridded vision, reaching down a gloved hand to help him up.

"You've got to keep your head up, Russ," Greg said as Russ regained his feet. They skated over to the box together and climbed over the wall, switching out with fresh players. "You know that; you've got the best vision of anyone on the ice. What's going on? You've been playing like a 'pod all night."

"'Pod" was short for *tripod*, a novice player who used his hockey stick like a third leg. "My head's not in the game," Russ admitted.

Greg thumped Russ's helmet with his stick. "Get it in the game or you're going to get hurt."

He was right; injuries happened when you weren't paying full attention. In their thirty-five-and-over amateur hockey league, injuries were scrupulously avoided. One bad knee blowout could end your days on the ice forever.

It was Emma Mayson who was screwing up his game. Since yesterday's wild conversation, he hadn't been able to concentrate on *anything* except the accidental agreement they'd made.

Today at work Kevin had glumly announced that Emma had canceled their date, since she was moving to a new apartment. She'd refused his offers of help, and refused to set up another date. Kevin had vowed to keep trying, anyway.

Russ had given a one-shoulder shrug. It wasn't as if he could tell his friend, "Don't feel bad. The real reason she canceled is so that I can pay her for sex three times a week."

Christ.

With great effort he kept his focus for the remaining ten minutes of the game, but as soon as it was over and he was heading to the locker room, his thoughts went back to Emma. The other guys were laughing and bantering about the game, giving each other a hard time and reliving the highs and lows as they showered and dressed, cans of Labatt's beer appearing out of gear bags and getting tossed to eager hands. It was all white noise.

Why the hell hadn't he cleared things up the moment he realized she thought he wanted her to be his mistress? The words had been halfway out his mouth before a voice inside had stopped him. *She's already agreed to it,* the voice said. She'd be humiliated if he told her he'd only meant to have dinner three times a week, not sex.

He'd thought that the best way to save her from embarrassment was to wait a few days and then tell her that he'd changed his mind and only wanted her to cook for him. He'd say that his conscience had bothered him, and that he could tell that she didn't truly want to do it.

All of which sounded well and good, but why, then, had he made an appointment to see his doctor and get a physical?

She's already agreed to it, the wicked voice said again. It hadn't been clear that she didn't want to do it either; in fact, there were moments during their "cooking" negotiations when he'd thought she was coming on to him. That made perfect sense, now that he knew her mind hadn't been on pot roasts.

He felt a hand on his shoulder and looked up.

"Are you going to put that sock on or just fondle it?" Greg said.

Russ looked down at the sock in his hand. He was fully dressed except for one foot, and a quick look around the locker room showed that most of the other guys had already left, headed over to Harold's Tavern for a more in-depth rehash of the game and colder beer.

"I fondle it, but it just lies there," Russ said.

Greg laughed. "You've got to spend more time with women. Are you coming to Harold's?"

"Yeah." Dwelling on the Emma situation wasn't making it any better, so maybe avoiding it would help.

The Harold of Harold's Tavern was eighty-five and possessed an even dozen Lincoln Continentals, all of which took up the front lot of the tavern, forcing patrons to park around the side. Harold himself was a thin man with fluffy white hair and pink skin that shone with cleanliness. The bar's half-block proximity to the ice arena made it the favorite hangout of the hockey players despite its being an utter dive.

A faded life-size cardboard cutout of Kathy Ireland in a bikini shared space with a 1970s big-screen TV, its blue projection light the only one still working. One corner of the bar was inexplicably filled with junk for sale, everything from a hot dog vending cart to a bright green lamp in the shape of a palm tree, a brown plastic monkey clinging to its side. Two pool tables got infrequent use, and most patrons eschewed seats at the U-shaped bar for the faux–wood grain Formica topped tables and brown vinyl-padded conference room chairs that took up what space remained. Several of the tables had been haphazardly pushed together for the use of the players.

For Russ, hockey and Harold's were like family and home, albeit in a peculiarly male fashion. You knew your teammates were there for you on the ice, watching your back, and here at Harold's they valued your company without wanting to know too much about you. It was an unwritten code among men that the less you knew about the guys you liked to do things with, the better. If you got to know them too well you might discover they were assholes, and then there went your fun.

When James had died, sympathy from the guys had been of the slap-on-the-back—"Hey man, I'm really sorry" and "I've been there"—variety, jaws set against remembered pain of their own. And then they talked about hockey, giving Russ the distraction that he needed and allowing him to keep his grief behind the facade of "dealing with it."

Greg was the only one he'd talked to about it in any depth. Their friendship went beyond the hours at the rink and Harold's: Russ had been best man at Greg's wedding eight years earlier and was godparent to one of his two kids. So as the evening wore down, it was to Greg that Russ finally said, "I have a date next Friday."

Greg put his beer down. "No fucking way!"

"It's a mistake."

Russ could never reveal to anyone the exact nature of his relationship with Emma, but even without the mistress factor there were plenty of issues. "She's ten years younger than me."

"So what?"

"Have *you* ever dated anyone that much younger?"

"Once. She made me feel like an old man. She listened to music I'd never heard of."

"So you see my problem."

Greg waved away his words. "Who needs music? Is she hot?"

"Yes."

"Then go for it! I'm married now. I have to get my thrills vicariously."

"Oh, shut up," Russ said. "Your wife is beautiful and about the sweetest woman I've ever met. It's a miracle she has the patience to put up with you." Greg's talk was all for show; Russ had never met a man who loved his wife as much as Greg loved his.

"It's obvious why she likes you. You take her side." Greg took a sip of beer. "So how'd you meet the hottie?"

"My sister hired her to clean my house," Russ said.

Greg laughed. "You've got to be kidding me. Fishing off your own dock, huh?"

"She's not going to clean my house anymore. But, er."

Greg raised his brows, waiting.

Russ sighed. "I rented my old apartment to her."

Greg's mouth dropped open. Several speechless moments went by, and then, "She must be fucking gorgeous."

"I thought I was helping out. Then suddenly we had a date planned, which I didn't want, and now I have to find a way to get out of it without hurting her feelings."

"Why do you want to get out of it?"

"She's ten years younger! She lives in a completely different world. She's immature. She's trying to find her place in the world."

"And she's hot. Let's not forget that she's hot."

Russ rolled his eyes.

"That's why you're talking to me," Greg said. "You know it's hopeless, but she's hot and you want her."

"If that thought doesn't make me want to break it off with her, nothing will. I don't want to be a creepy old fart."

"Stop being so hard on yourself. Frankly, I'm proud of you."

"*What?*"

Greg sat back, crossed one ankle over his knee, and said in an expansive, professorial tone, "It means you're getting on with life. And what a way to get on with it!"

"You're not much help."

"You don't *want* help. You want someone to validate your choice to jump her. You want to be absolved of guilt for being a lech."

Russ scowled. "I have to cancel this date."

Greg put his foot back on the floor, leaning forward and slapping both palms onto the table. "Don't do that, Russ," he pleaded. "You're living the dream, man! You're single, you're rich, and now you've got a hot young thing eager to jump your bones. You *have* to let her. Keep living the dream! For me. For your teammates. For every man who wishes he still had all his hair, a thirty-inch waist, and sex without begging."

Greg turned toward their teammate Tom, a forty-six-year-old accountant sitting at the other end of the row of tables. "Tom! Tell Russ what your wife did last week!"

"She went down on me," Tom said, a note of awe in his voice. His eyes gleamed as if recounting a visit by a saint. "For the first time in three years. And I didn't even ask. It was a beautiful thing." He touched the corner of one eye and made a noise suspiciously like a tear being sniffed back. "Beautiful."

Greg nodded at Russ. "You see? Three years without a blow job. That's what the future holds."

"You're depressing me," Russ said. "This is what life holds?"

"You're the last of the wild cowboys. We look at you as our symbol of freedom. That's why everyone's wife tries to set you up, marry you off. They want to take away our hope. They want us to forget that we, too, once ran free."

"Then why do we all end up married in the end? Why aren't the lot of you out roaming the range?"

"Gotta have someone to take care of me when I'm old," Tom said from down the table. "I already got arthritis in one foot. High cholesterol, bowel troubles—*bad* bowel troubles. Who's going to take care of me *but* my wife?"

Russ dropped his face into his hands, shaking his head. "More than I wanted to know, Tom. More than I wanted to know."

"Of course, the wife's the one who's making me go in for that colonoscopy." Tom scowled into his beer. "I'm not sure a blow job makes up for a camera up my ass."

"You see?" Greg said, his face a mask of pathos. "You

gotta run free. For all of us. Seize the hottie, I say! Seize the hottie!"

"I'm too young for a midlife crisis. I'm breaking the date."

"Traitor."

Russ shook his head and promised himself he'd call Emma first thing in the morning and cancel their arrangement.

Six

Emma looked at the clock and whimpered. Russ would be there in fifteen minutes and she wasn't ready. *Nothing* was ready! Her eyes went to the microwave and the sexual accessory waiting within it.

Okay, so *one* thing was ready. But everything else was a disaster! It had been a week since she moved into the apartment, yet somehow that hadn't been enough time to get ready for this night.

She'd been late getting the stuffed, boneless leg of lamb into the oven and it still had forty minutes to cook, plus another fifteen minutes to rest before she could cut it, according to the recipe she'd downloaded off epicurious.com. The lima bean puree with garlic and rosemary had been made ahead and waited now to be rewarmed, but the utensils she had used were piled on the counter and in the sink, and her immersion blender had flung gobs of green puree onto the backsplash, the cupboards, and her blouse. The mint truffle ice-cream terrine for dessert was safely in the freezer, the homemade chocolate sauce in the fridge, but the mint sauce that also went with it was no more than a bag of leaves at the moment.

The table was only half-set. Her hair and face were a mess. Her *body* was a mess, the shower she'd taken earlier now a distant, sweaty memory.

She took a deep breath, assessing the situation. The lamb was cooking on its own. Setting the table and making the mint sauce could wait. The mixed greens salad was ready to throw together, giving him something to eat while she finished everything else up. If she was going to clean herself up, though, now was her only chance.

She looked down at her hands, which were shaking. Now that she was pausing in her frantic cooking rush she realized that her gut was sloshing with acid, her heart irregularly thumping, her vision blurring from the overdose of adrenaline.

The nervous anticipation was worse than on any first date. It was even worse than the night she lost her virginity.

Am I really going to do this? Am I really going to let a man I hardly know have sex with me three times a week?

She hovered on the thin edge of indecision, swaying between telling Russ to forget it, it was a mistake, she had to have been crazy to have said yes, and going ahead with the arrangement.

Is this really what I want?

68

She imagined the evening: Russ eating the dinner she'd made and then looking at her, silence falling between them as they both recognized that the time had come. She would send him to her bedroom while she prepared for the sexual experiment she'd downloaded off the internet; he'd said to be creative, after all. The activity was nothing she herself had ever done and at the thought of it, her body fluttered between arousal and the fear of humiliation. Russ might be turned off by it, and she might end up looking the fool. But if it worked . . .

At the end of it she would climb on top of him, her thighs parting over his hips, and guide the tip of his hardened shaft to her opening. She'd feel herself stretching as she eased herself down on him, his erection filling her as she had longed to be filled for so many lonely months, and then his hands would come up to grip her hips and guide her to his own rocking, thrusting motion.

Oh yes. A warm rush went through her loins. *Yes,* this was what she wanted, nerves be damned! And let the opinions of others be damned as well!

Emma tossed down her oven mitts and dashed for the bathroom to give herself a sponge bath and slap on some makeup. Sitting on the back of the toilet tank was the cold-waxing kit she'd bought earlier in the week and had conveniently forgotten about. She stared at it. She lifted her short skirt and looked down, parting her thighs enough to see if it was really so bad that she needed the wax.

Holy hairy monkeys!

She couldn't show that tangle to him. Couldn't send his penis fighting through that thicket, with its dark curls creeping down the insides of her thighs like vines.

She'd shaved inside her thighs before, but it always left sharp stubble and a rash. If she was going to be someone's lust object, she wanted to be smooth and sleek and not worried about whether he was going to get sandpapered by her thighs.

She stripped and gave herself a quick sponge bath, put on some red lipstick as the quickest way to brighten up her face, combed her hair and smoothed out the frizzies with water and silicone serum, then sat on the edge of the tub and tore into the wax kit.

The instructions were full of cautions, but she'd waxed her legs a few years ago and figured she understood the basics. The cold wax came in a tube and had the consistency of honey. She squeezed a blob of it onto the small plastic spatula from the kit, smeared it over a quarter-sized patch of hair inside her thigh, pressed a strip of cloth over it, then held her skin taut with one hand while ripping off the cloth with the other.

"Holy crap!" she screeched, and slapped one palm down over her offended flesh, hoping that pressure would ease the pain. A moment later she lifted her hand and examined the damage. Her skin bore faint pink dots where each hair had been exhumed, but was otherwise a smooth, lovely patch of civilized hairlessness amid the wilds.

Emma darted naked out into the kitchen and checked

the time: she had eight minutes. She darted back into the bathroom, hoping Russ would be late.

If she waxed in sensible one-inch patches it would take her forever to get it done, and impatience drove her to slather progressively wider and longer strips of wax on her skin, press on the cloth, then pull it off in a series of short jerks. Stray dollops of wax attached to her fingers, to the tub, to hairs she didn't intend to pull.

The doorbell rang and her hand jerked, sending a smear of wax from her inner thigh into the hair on her mound. "Dammit!" With the spatula she tried to scrape the wax off, but it made things worse. She took a cloth and slapped it down on the mess of wax.

He knocked on the door.

"I'm coming! One second!" she shouted, and tried to rip the cloth off. "*Monkey Christ!*" she shrieked, and tumbled in pain to the bathroom floor, her thighs clamped shut over the agony.

"Emma?" Russ called from the other side of the front door, his voice muffled.

"I'm okay!" she squeaked. "I'll be right there!"

She lay for a moment, breathing heavily and waiting for the pain to fade, then pushed herself up into a sitting position and looked at her crotch. The white cloth was attached to her like a bandage, running diagonally across her mound and down between her thighs. She lifted up the top corner and gave it a little jerk.

"Jeee-zus H!"

There was too much wax and way too much hair. She snatched up the instruction sheet, scanning it for what to do. She turned it over, then turned back to the other side. Where did it say what to do? Where?

"Emma?" Russ called again.

"Dammit! Dammit dammit dammit!" She'd have to figure it out later. She grabbed all the waxing paraphernalia and shoved it into the cabinet under the sink. She got up off the floor and yelped as she tried to straighten up. The damn wax and cloth had glued her left leg into a raised position. Standing up straight stretched her skin painfully. "Crap!" She'd have to hide her limp as best she could. She pulled on her bra, sleeveless white blouse, and short green skirt, skipping the underpants. She didn't want *those* stuck to her as well.

With the waxed cloth tugging painfully with each uneven stride, she hobbled barefoot to the front door and put her hand on the knob. She rested her weight on her right leg, the left one cocked and on tiptoe, as if it were a sultry pose. She took a deep breath and tried to calm herself, and planted a welcoming smile on her lips.

Ready or not, here she was.

Russ approached the door to his old apartment with an unsettling mix of familiarity and alienness. It had been home to him for several years, but never in that time had there been a woman behind that door with dinner waiting and the intention of taking him to her bed. As wrong as he intellectually knew this arrangement was, as wrong as he emotionally *felt* that it was, part of him wanted it the way a drowning man wanted to see a ship in the distance. It might be an illusion, but what a beautiful illusion it was.

And *wrong!* Wrong, wrong, wrong, he reminded himself. All week, he had meant to call Emma and break their agreement. He'd meant to do that even as he express-mailed her a loaded Visa card. He'd meant to do it as he e-mailed her a link to his lab test results. He'd meant to do it as he bought a bouquet for her, walked into the building, and rode up the elevator—and now, as he stood before his old door, he still meant to do it.

He looked at the flowers. What the hell was he thinking? This wasn't a date!

But what *was* it? His mind scrambled back through memory, trying to find a parallel. All he could think of was Madame de Pompadour, the eighteenth-century mistress to the French king. He didn't doubt that she was given flowers. Jewels, likely. Clothes, even land. Aristocrats used to give their mistresses houses and land, didn't they?

His cellophane-wrapped Dutch irises from Pike Place Market suddenly looked inadequate.

But wait, the flowers were an apology for asking her to be his mistress, then recanting.

Weren't they?

He wished he had a beer.

He reached up and rang the bell.

Nothing happened. No footsteps, no replying voice. He knocked.

"I'm coming! One second!" she called, and then he heard a shrieking curse and a big thump.

"Emma?" he called in alarm.

She squeaked something he couldn't make out, then said, "I'll be right there."

More silence. More muffled cursing. Silence again.

"Emma?" he called carefully, imagining all sorts of mishaps. Maybe she'd hit her head and was disoriented. Maybe she'd cut herself. Maybe—

He heard her approach the door and then stop. A quiet fell in which he imagined he could hear her taking a breath. He stared at the wall of door, knowing she was there.

Then she opened the door.

She was gorgeous. Her fair skin was flushed pink, her rosy lips parted in a welcoming smile. Her brown eyes sparkled and her dark hair fell like mink around her shoulders. His gaze skimmed down her body, taking in the vee of her blouse and the barest hint of lacy bra showing at one edge. Her short, emerald green pleated skirt looked like something a naughty Irish schoolgirl might wear. Her legs and feet were bare, one leg cocked enticingly, the lack of shoes making her seem more accessible.

His mouth went dry. This beautiful young woman was going to take him to her bed tonight. He imagined those soft pink lips on his arousal, those bright dark eyes looking up at him as she took him into her mouth. Lust stirred within him, his sex hardening.

"This was a mistake," he said, and thrust the flowers toward her.

"Nonsense! They're beautiful," she said, taking the bouquet. She sniffed them. "Thank you. Although I can't smell them over the roasting lamb." She lowered the flowers to chest height and smiled at him. "Come in, please. Dinner is almost ready."

He followed her reluctantly, wanting to correct her about what the mistake had been, but he was distracted by both the delicious scent of roasting meat and Emma's odd hopping gait. "Did you hurt yourself?"

"Just a temporary muscle tightness. Nothing to worry about!" She lurched into the kitchen.

He was going to ask again about her leg—it seemed a severe muscle issue—but was distracted by what she had done with his old place. The kitchen and living area were one room, divided only by a high breakfast bar. She had created a third space in the bay window at the front of the apartment by hanging panels of salvaged wood-framed windows from floor to ceiling, dividing the bay from the living area. She'd set up a dining area in that small glass-enclosed space, a tablecloth covering what looked like a card table. Two of the bay windows were open, bringing in the rustling of the leaves just outside them. It was surprisingly charming.

The living area had a futon couch, a desk with an elaborate array of computer equipment, a drafting table, and a bookshelf sagging with the weight of tomes. The only art on the walls was a series of black-and-white architectural photographs in lucite frames.

"These are fantastic pictures," he said, pausing to admire the light and shadow in an arched gallery.

"Thanks. I took them."

He turned, surprised. "You're a photographer, too?"

She shrugged and took the cellophane off the irises and started trimming their stems. "Not really. I only take them for myself, and they're only of things that I find beautiful. Patterns, mostly. Repetition. Symmetry. Angles and curves."

"The mathematics of beauty."

She looked up from filling a vase and smiled. "Yes. Exactly. Most people don't get that; that there is math in both the visual arts and music."

"You're talking to an engineer."

She laughed. "I guess that could explain it, but I've met plenty of math and science guys who lack an aesthetic sense. Look at the great flowers you chose: structural, and all one kind. I think it's the best way to display flowers."

Flattered, he made a faint noise that might be construed as thanks.

"So!" she said brightly. "Would you like to open the wine?" She put a bottle of red up on the breakfast bar, then bumped it when she reached up again to put down the corkscrew. She fumbled and just managed to catch it before it fell over, and before his own mad dash got him there. "Oops! Sometimes I think I'm all thumbs," she said, a quaver in her voice. She giggled, but not a happy giggle. More a verge-of-hysteria giggle.

He reached for the wine bottle and corkscrew and examined her surreptitiously as he went to work on the bottle.

Emma hopped about the small kitchen, prattling something about micro salad greens and vinegars, her hands moving as fast as birds' wings.

He pulled the cork and moved to her side of the breakfast bar, where the wineglasses were. He poured out two glasses, glad to see no cork bits, and paused to look at the wine label. It was a nice pinot noir from Oregon.

She bumped into him and bounced away, his closeness seeming to make her hummingbird nervousness go up a notch.

He reached out and touched her arm, to calm her, to tell her that she didn't have to do this. "It's okay," he said.

Her eyes went past him to the wine. "Is it? I was hoping so. I'm afraid I don't know as much as I'd like to about wine. The woman at the wine shop down the block chose it for me."

She snatched a glass and held it up. "Here's to new adventures!"

He took a glass as well, but when she clinked her glass with his he didn't drink. "Emma."

She lowered her glass. He saw faint tremors in the surface of her wine, revealing the shaking of her hand. "Yes?"

"You don't have to do this. We can stop right here. Forget the whole arrangement."

Her eyebrows went up in concern. "Stop? You've changed your mind? You don't want any of this?"

"It's not right."

"But I made a stuffed leg of lamb. And dessert." She looked helplessly around the kitchen, the signs of her efforts clear in the dirty bowls, pans, and utensils.

"We can still eat the dinner you made. Maybe even make a deal for you to cook at my house a couple times a week. But I don't want you to feel like you have to follow through on the rest."

Some of the light left her eyes. She looked *hurt*. "You don't want to sleep with me."

"Yes! I do! But you're so nervous, I wanted to give you a chance to reconsider." *He* was calling *her* nervous. Ha! What a joke! He was the one who was ready to die of nerves.

She set down her wineglass and played with its base, watching her own fingertips sliding around the circle of glass. Then she suddenly looked up, meeting his eyes with a steady gaze. "It's been a year and a half since I've had sex. They say it's like riding a bicycle and you never forget how, right? But that doesn't mean there isn't a part of me that's still a little nervous, no matter how much I'm looking forward to it."

He was surprised and pleased by her admissions of having been celibate for so long and of wanting to sleep with him. "It's been a while for me, too," he said quietly.

"I've never done it with someone I wasn't in a long-term relationship with." She stepped closer to him, bringing her mouth within inches of his own. "And I've never been creative with it, before tonight. But it's good to try new things. To learn. Don't you think?"

He could feel the warmth of her breath against his lips. "Education is important." He tried to give nobility one last chance. "I don't want to corrupt you."

"The sin of knowledge? A bit old school, don't you think?"

"I don't want you to be ashamed, afterwards."

"Will *you* think badly of me, if I become your mistress?"

Would he think less of her if she went through with it? If she were his age or looking for marriage, then he might. But Emma had other things on her mind than relationships. From what little he knew of her, she wouldn't be doing this unless it made practical and moral sense to her.

He laughed as he realized what his answer to her question was. "If you go through with it, tomorrow I'll wonder if it's all been real."

She raised a brow. "Will I be a toy to you? A sex toy in a very large toy box?" She gestured to the apartment.

"Not a toy. A toy implies mastery by another. I think

'pagan goddess' would be the better description. A goddess bestowing gifts upon the incredibly fortunate."

She smiled and came close enough for her lips to brush his. "I can live with that."

He was suddenly sure that he could, too. Oh God, yes, he could. He put his hand on her hip and began to close the scant distance.

The buzz of the oven timer cut between them. "Oh good, there's the lamb!" she said, hopping away from him and grabbing her oven mitts.

"Hurrah," he muttered. Walking was becoming difficult for *him* now, as well. He moved to the other side of the breakfast bar, where his lower half would be out of sight.

He watched her lift the pan out of the oven. She glanced up at him and smiled, and for the first time in his life he seriously wondered if he should start looking for a wife. There was something deeply appealing about a woman cooking for you. Though this was only a business arrangement, it was easy to forget that fact when Emma smiled at him, when she seemed to take such care and delight in the meal she had made.

"Do you want to help?" she asked.

"Sure. What do you need me to do?"

"You could finish setting the table. I took out dishes for two settings, if that's okay."

He looked at her in puzzlement.

"I wasn't sure that you'd want me to eat with you, or if this was supposed to be more like a restaurant experience."

"Two places is what I expected," he said, although he hadn't given it a thought before this moment. He couldn't swallow a bite if she was hovering in the background, watching.

"Good! I'm starving."

He went to work on the table. As he was finishing up she hobbled up to join him, carrying two plates of salad. He went back and got the wine, returning to find her lighting candles. It was a much more romantic setting than he had anticipated, and he was glad for it. It gave the illusion that they were both here because they wanted to be.

And wasn't that true anyway?

Emma stood in her awkward bird pose beside the table, gesturing toward a chair. "Sit. Please."

He moved past her and pulled out the other chair for her. "Please," he said. She might soon be his mistress, but that didn't mean he couldn't be a gentleman about it.

She ducked her head shyly and sat as he pushed in the chair.

"Your leg is still bothering you," he said.

"It'll go away, don't worry."

"Are you sure?"

"Oh, yes."

He took his own seat, still doubtful. "Do you need me to massage it?"

The suggestion made her eyes go wide. "No! No, really, there's no need to bother."

"I have strong hands: I could take care of it in a flash. It'll be gone before you know it."

She grimaced. "I doubt that. Trust me, it's going to be fine. Let's have our salads, shall we?"

He let it go, turning his attention to his plate. It was mixed baby greens with thin slices of pear, crumbled gorgonzola, and candied pecans. He'd had something similar in a restaurant, and Emma's version was just as good. "This is delicious."

"Thanks."

After this scintillating start, conversation lagged. Russ racked his brain to come up with something that might be of interest to a twenty-six-year-old woman.

Twenty-six-year-old? He couldn't come up with anything to say to a woman, period. His life revolved around work, hockey, a bit of charity fund-raising, and sitting in his recliner reading the paper. He couldn't remember the last time he'd done anything significantly different. He used to have hobbies: he used to play classical guitar; used to play a mean game of backgammon; used to camp and hike and had backpacked around Europe and southeast Asia for six months; he even used to dink around in his wood shop, making bad furniture.

Emma made a little noise in her throat, and he realized that the silence had gone for much longer than it should have. "Shall I put on some music?" she asked.

"Sure." Anything to fill up the silence. It would probably

be teeny bopper music that he'd never heard. Just as long as it wasn't rap or hip-hop.

When she'd chosen a few disks and pressed play, though, Dean Martin's "Sway" came out of the small speakers.

He laughed. "This is way before my generation. I hope you don't think I'm that old!"

"Stop with the 'old' stuff, will you?" she said, sitting down again. "You're in your freakin' thirties. Big deal."

"I stand corrected."

"Good." She smiled. "And I happen to like old standards, and this song in particular."

"It's a great song."

"My mother used to play it and dance 'round the living room with our pomeranian in her arms. I'm not sure the dog thought much of the experience. It was a terrible dog; peed on everything."

"So your mother loves Dean Martin?"

"She says it was 'their' song, hers and my dad's. He died when I was nine."

"I'm so sorry." He imagined her mother dancing around the living room with the lapdog in her arms, swaying to the voice of Dean Martin as she longed for her husband. The image cut to that part of him that still grieved for James, and he felt his throat tighten. "So sorry."

Emma shrugged, her smile sad. "Life's full of surprises."

"How's your mother now?"

"She remarried a few years ago and lives in the Midwest now. She's happy."

"It must have been hard for you, losing him at such a young age."

"It was bewildering. Frightening. Mostly I remember the feeling of chaos; that all normality had been destroyed. I was afraid we'd have to move."

"Did you?"

"No. Grandma came to live with us. She somehow made us all feel safe; that things were going to be okay. And we were, mostly. My brother got into a lot of trouble at school and had a few wild years, but he turned out okay. He lives in Kirkland now, with his wife and baby daughter."

"Is your grandmother still around?"

She shook her head. "She died a couple years ago."

"That's a lot of death to have experienced, for someone as young as you."

"I think it helps me to appreciate the present. At least I tell myself it does. What about you? Have you lost anyone you cared about?"

"My brother. Six months ago." He somehow managed to get the words out.

"What was his name?"

"James." To his horror he felt tears start in his eyes. He cleared his throat. "But this isn't pleasant dinner conversation. I think the lamb must be ready."

She looked at him for a long moment with wordless understanding, got up and lightly touched the back of his hand, then reached for his plate.

"I'll get it," he said, starting to stand.

"No, you can relax. Let me."

He stayed where he was, the feeling of that small touch on his hand lingering. As he watched her move away with the salad plates he yearned to sink into the warmth she seemed to offer; wanted to forget himself in her, if only for a few hours. Something about her seemed capable of that type of magic, transforming the grayness of his everyday life into something brighter.

The rest of the meal passed with light conversation about the city, about where they grew up, about places they'd been in the world. She'd spent her junior year of college in Italy and traveled extensively while she was there, which gave them plenty of impersonal topics to explore. They moved through the meal and into dessert: a mint truffle ice-cream terrine with two sauces.

"My God, you made this?" he asked as she set the square slice of ice cream with truffle polka dots in front of him.

"It wasn't as hard as it looks." She launched into a rapid-fire description of the construction, her voice higher than it had been over the lamb and side dish.

It took him a couple minutes to figure out what was going on. The instant he did, her nervousness became contagious. Once the ice cream was finished it would be time for that other "dessert."

Dammit! He'd forgotten about that—a testament to her cooking, or to his powers of denial.

Would she expect him to take the lead? No, wait. She'd said something about being creative with sex.

Crap. What did *creative* mean?

B movies rife with whip-wielding dominatrices cracked through his mind. Or maybe she'd bought a frightening toy at a sex shop: something long and electric, with nubs and lights and six speeds of humiliation.

He only had three bites of ice cream left until he was going to find out.

He made those last three bites last as long as he could, then looked at his watch. Eight-thirty. The night was young. Plenty of time for whatever she had planned.

Oh God.

"It's time, isn't it?" Emma asked, her voice going up two octaves.

"For coffee?" he asked, pretending ignorance. Hoping she would take the stall.

"Coffee breath," she said. "Although I suppose we could brush. Only you didn't bring a toothbrush, did you?"

Oh God. Did he have bad breath? Was there food in his teeth? "No. I could go out and buy one."

"Easier to save the coffee for later, don't you think?" she asked with a quaver. "I imagine you'll, uh, be sleepy. Afterwards. And you have to drive home."

"Sleepy. Yes." Ah jeez, she meant after he'd come. Oh God. Oh God.

"You *were* planning to go home afterwards, weren't you?"

"God, yes. I wouldn't want to intrude."

She giggled. "No. We wouldn't want that. No intrusions of any sort!"

"Emma—" he started.

"No," she said, cutting him off. She took a deep breath, regaining her composure. "Don't say it again. I *want* to do this. If you need to use the bathroom, please go ahead and do so. Then I'd appreciate it if you'd go into my bedroom, undress, and lie on the bed. I have something special planned: the 'something big' you said you wanted on Fridays, to last you through the weekend."

All I meant was a nice casserole.

"Okay." He went to clean up in the bathroom with all the enthusiasm of a man preparing himself for the guillotine.

When he came out, she was leaving the bedroom. They sidled past each other in the short hall. He went into his former bedroom, dominated now by a queen-size antique brass bed, its covers folded down to the foot revealing a white expanse of crisp, clean sheet. Candles in small glass votives covered the dresser and bedside tables. The furniture and a cheval mirror were all antiques: like the dishes, they must have been inherited from her grandmother.

The thought threw more water on his already damp

amour. He didn't want to think of Grandma looking down from her heavenly abode at what was happening to her granddaughter on her bed.

That didn't stop him from undressing. He heard Emma go into the bathroom. She clearly wanted to do this; apparently was looking forward to it, and that, as much as his own awareness that he was not quite so reluctant as he pretended to himself, made him fold up his clothes and leave them in a neat pile on the floor beside the dresser.

He climbed onto the bed and lay down, his head on a pillow. After a moment he found the position too vulnerable, and stacked up all the pillows behind him so that he could sit up. He crossed his arms over his chest.

His penis lay half-tumescent as if it, too, was not sure if this was going to be a good experience.

He wished he had something to cover it with.

He heard a curse through the bathroom wall, right behind his head. Then another curse and movement. What the hell was she doing in there?

He perked his ears, listening. She must not know how easy it was to hear through these walls.

"Ow!" she said. "Ow! Dammit! Ow!"

His eyes widened. Visions of nipple clips and leather-wrapped objects for insertion into various orifices danced in his head.

Emma muttered darkly and thumped around a bit; then there was an ominous silence. His ears strained, trying to pick up some hint of what was happening. The silence continued. If he hadn't known better, he would have thought there was no one there.

And then all at once the silence was split by a *Hai-ya!* and a brief ripping sound. He bolted upright, his semiarousal shrinking like a snail withdrawing into its shell. There was a slap and a squeak, and then all was quiet again except for the pounding of his heart.

The water ran and was shut off, and a minute later the bathroom door opened. He grabbed the sheet at the bottom of the bed and pulled it up over his hips as he lay back, trying desperately to look relaxed.

"Almost ready!" she called softly. "Are you?"

"Sure." He swallowed and gathered his courage. He didn't want to disappoint her or hurt her feelings; somehow, no matter what she had planned, he was going to have to perform.

He tried to imagine her bare breasts. Touching one. Licking the nipples.

He heard the microwave turn on.

The microwave? What the hell was she doing with the microwave? She wasn't heating up a dildo, was she?

He closed his eyes and tried to think happy, bouncing-booby thoughts. He reached down and shook his penis, trying to encourage it to return to life. A shrunken willie was not the first naked impression a man wanted to give a woman.

The microwave stopped, the door opened and closed. Then the music that had been playing stopped and he heard her changing disks. The *pianissimo* opening bars of Ravel's *Bolero* began to filter into the bedroom. His penis perked up. It was the music used to cheesy sexual effect in the old Bo Derek movie, the piece composed of the same few bars of exotic, swaying melody repeated ad infinitum, only slightly louder each time as if building to a climax. Cheesy, but very promising.

He sensed Emma approaching. He pulled his hands back above the sheet and opened his eyes.

She was standing in the doorway, a red mixing bowl in her hands. She wore black fishnet stockings, a tiny white apron, and a small white cap pinned atop her head. His gaze skimmed over her body, seeking out piercings and straps of leather buckling on latex appendages. Relieved to find none, he took a slower, more appreciative look, his sex reviving as he took in the fall of her dark hair against the smooth paleness of her shoulders; the gentle fullness of her breasts with their pinkish brown nipples; the slope and rise of her waistline; the hint of black curls imperfectly concealed behind that little apron that he now guessed was meant to be an abbreviated French maid's outfit.

His animal lust shoved his noble instincts firmly to the back of his mind.

"What's in the bowl?" he asked, half-hopeful and half-wary.

Emma concentrated on keeping her hands from shaking as she stood in the doorway, the warm bowl in her hands and the apron the only shelter from his gaze. She had seen his eyes surf over her body, once quickly and then again more slowly. He gave no indication of whether he liked what he saw. Her gaze skimmed over his chest and shoulders; he was even more fit than she had guessed, his muscles well defined and coating his frame in a thicker, more solid layer than she'd seen on men her own age. He looked like a man, not a boy. Brown hair lightly covered his pectorals and traced a line toward his navel. She'd never been with someone with chest hair, and there was something about it in this context that made her nervous; it made her more aware that she was here to please a man, not to play with a boy.

"You'll find out soon enough what's in the bowl," she said, arching a brow and trying to sound confidently mischievous.

"Before you find out what's in the bowl you have to agree to two rules," she said, trying to stick to the plan for a "blow his mind" evening she'd downloaded from a sex advice site on the Internet.

"Okay," he said warily.

"The first is that you can't come until I say you can. No matter what I'm doing and how much you enjoy it, you can't come until I say so."

The sheet over his loins moved, a mound forming. "Okay."

"And two: you can't touch me until I say you can. You have to let me do to you exactly what I want."

The mound turned into a ridge, tenting the sheet. "I think I can do that."

She grinned, her confidence rising along with his erection.

She came forward and rested the bowl against her hip as she reached down and slowly pulled the sheet off him. The head of his erection came free, and then the whole lusty rod in its entirety, thick and strong and rising proudly from a dark thicket of hair, his balls beneath drawn tight up against his body. His thighs were lightly coated with dark hair, the hair growing heavier farther down his legs and ending neatly at the top of his pale, clean feet.

"You look like a satyr," she said.

"Is that good or bad?"

She felt a tingling between her thighs as anticipated being taken by him, those strong thighs between her own softer ones, that rigid member embedded deep within her. "It's good," she said in a husky voice. "Definitely good."

She set the bowl down on the side of the bed and dipped a finger in. She put on a fake French accent to go with her outfit. "Do you like zee chocolate?"

"Usually," he said warily. "Why?"

Emma had never been an actress; she couldn't even lie. As her finger scooped up a dollop of warm chocolate pudding, embarrassment made her want to giggle and make a joke about the situation; she was afraid that he would find what she was about to do ridiculous instead of sexy.

"Vhy? Because you are about to have a très intimate encounter with it." She lifted the dollop of pudding and, with her eyes locked on his, painted it around her left nipple.

His eyes dropped to her breast, watching the movement. She swirled it over her aureole, leaving the peak of her nipple bare, then brought her finger to her mouth and slowly sucked the pudding off.

His erection bobbed in approval. "I think that chocolate just became my favorite food."

A smile quavered on her lips. A good start, but it was ad-lib time now. The sex advice script hadn't filled in all the blanks for this amorous scene, and she'd never been naturally creative with her body movements. She didn't even dance.

She dipped her finger again into the pudding and circled her other nipple, nervousness making her do it too quickly. She *knew* she was too fast, too stiff, but she couldn't stop herself. With more pudding she drew an outward spiral over her breast, watching her fingertip to make sure she got the spiral perfect. The shaking of her hand made the line wobbly. She scowled and tried to correct it, licking her finger and wiping off the uneven bits.

She glanced up at Russ and saw a faint frown between his brows, the delight of a minute before now fading, his erection looking a hair less upright. She was losing her audience. She was doing a terrible job of being seductive.

A squeaky giggle of embarrassment slipped out. "I'm messing this up." She fluttered her hands helplessly in the air. "Do you want me to stop this? This pudding thing?"

"No. But . . ."

"But?"

"If I could offer a word of advice?"

"Please!"

"Go slow. And drop the accent."

She blushed. "Okay." She could do slow, couldn't she? And dropping the accent was easy enough. He didn't want her to stop *everything*. Just to slow down.

She closed her eyes and listened to the music. The rhythm was slow and swaying; she could imagine a belly dancer moving to it. Opening her eyes she set her gaze high up on the wall, so that Russ was only a blur in her peripheral vision. She untied the apron and let it fall, then scooped up more of the warm pudding and painted a circle in the center of her torso with two fingers. Trying to forget that she was being watched, she swirled her fingertips in the dollop of pudding and then let them wander across her skin in slow, dancing loops, moving with the beat of the music. She scrolled a path along the bottom of her ribs, letting the music guide her instincts, her fingertips dancing upward to paint the underside of one breast.

She let her fingers slide up over her nipple, the warm slickness of the pudding feeling erotic, turning her own fingertips into a warm tongue. She slid the peak of her nipple into the vee of two fingers, feeling the aroused hardness of it. She pinched it lightly and sensation shot straight down her body. Her lips parted and her breathing deepened.

With her other hand she dipped again into the bowl. She lowered her gaze to Russ, not afraid now to look at him. He was transfixed by her play with the chocolate, his gaze going back and forth between her nipple and her other hand, moving now toward her lower belly.

She smeared the chocolate just above her mound, then played at the tops of her thighs, creating a circle around her sex. She let her fingers go down into what remained of her hair, to smear the warm smoothness over the hood of her desire, stroking it while he watched and feeling the pleasure that came with her own touch. She had never touched herself in front of a man; had never let one watch as she gave herself pleasure. He clearly was enjoying the show, his attention never wavering.

She didn't see him now as the man she was here to please. He was the gorgeous male body she was going to use for her own delight. Her toy, her willing slave who did as she bid.

She climbed onto the bed, straddling him, and moved her hips back and forth over his erection, letting her folds lick his length, his rod massaging her clit as she moved over him. He reached up and held her hips, urging her down harder.

"Don't touch!" she ordered.

He groaned and dropped his hands.

She got down on all fours over him and lowered herself until she could feel his hardness pressing into the softness of her lower belly. She rubbed against him, the chocolate letting her glide over his ridge, then lowered herself farther so her nipples could rub against his chest. His hair tickled at her, stimulating her in a way she would never have guessed.

She glanced up and met his hazel eyes, the color almost swallowed by the blackness of his enlarged pupils. She wiped a bit of chocolate off her breast and painted it over his lower lip. He held motionless while she did, but she could hear his quickened breathing and feel his tension beneath her.

He's mine to do with as I please.

She licked the chocolate off his lip, then sucked at it, running her tongue over the soft silkiness. He started to kiss her back and she withdrew.

She slid down his body, letting her nipples rub against him the whole way, enjoying the feel of him beneath her. His erection slid neatly between her breasts, and that felt good, too. She raised her eyes to meet his gaze, then with gazes locked she pressed her hands to either side of her breasts and squeezed, trapping him between her mounds. Kneeling in a crouch, she raised and lowered her torso, pumping him between her breasts. He gasped, his rod sliding easily in the chocolate, the head popping out between the tops of her breasts at the end of each stroke.

"It feels so good," Emma said. "Feeling you against me, here."

"Oh God . . ."

"Don't come."

"Christ . . ."

She slid her hands so that her nipples peeked out from between her fingers as she pressed her breasts. That, too, felt good.

"Emma . . ."

"I'm not done." She released her breasts and slid lower down his body still, forcing his legs to part and give her someplace to crouch, his erection near her face. There was chocolate smeared all over him.

She licked one of his balls tentatively, not sure what she'd think of it. Chocolate and skin; a faint coat of hair.

She licked again, a little more firmly, enough to lightly splay her tongue against him and take off some of the chocolate.

"Emma, what are you doing?"

"You have chocolate all over you. I have to clean you up."

His answer was a long groan.

Grinning, she lowered her head and went to slow, methodical work, starting at the bottom and working her way upward over every inch. Swirling her tongue at the base of his rod; licking at its sides as if it were a melting ice-cream cone; then finally tracing the edge of his head with the point of her tongue and then rubbing her tongue hard against the spot facing her where head met length. She felt his body hardening, all his muscles tensing.

She rested her closed lips over the tip and parted them slightly to taste the first drop of his desire. She pressed downward, letting the force of her descent open her lips around him, his engorged head filling her mouth and forcing her tongue down. She kept her lips carefully over her teeth and took him until he hit the back of her mouth. She sucked and pulled off him, then went to it in earnest, wrapping her hand around his shaft and moving it up and down in synch with her mouth.

Russ's breathing grew louder and more ragged. He lifted his hands beside her head and she knew he wanted to grasp her, either to stop her or to move her deeper. But he held off, obeying her command not to touch.

She released his shaft and moved her hand down, lightly stroking his balls. His whole body clenched.

"Emma, you've got to stop. Please, Emma! I can't hold back any longer."

She released him, rising up on her knees to look down at him. He lay beneath her, panting. She dipped her finger again into the chocolate and painted one of her nipples, then the other, then slowly brought her finger to her mouth and sucked off what remained. "You can touch me now."

"Thank God!" Russ sat up and scooped her into his arms, then lay her down on the mattress. He lowered his mouth to her chocolate-coated nipple, sucking hungrily, rolling the bead of it against his tongue. She moaned.

Russ heard the moan and felt his crotch respond. He wanted to part her thighs and plunge into her right this moment; but if he did, it would be over in three thrusts. He knew he couldn't hold back much longer.

He laved her other nipple, cleaning it, and felt her raise her hips against him in a silent plea for him to enter her. She raised her knees, tilting her hips for greater contact between them. He licked his way down her torso, sliding his body between her legs, feeling the softness of her lower hair and the dampness of her own desire against his belly.

His need for her burned, but he refused to let his satisfaction arrive with a simple thrust. To slow himself down he moved yet farther down her body until he could slide his arms under her fishnet-clad thighs and bend them, his hands coming up to splay against her hips, holding her pelvis captive. Her sex was bare before him, easy prey to his hungry mouth.

"Russ, you don't have to," she said, reaching down and touching the side of his head.

Of course he didn't have to, but it was something he'd never particularly enjoyed with past girlfriends, so it would give him time to cool down. He lowered his mouth to her dark pink folds and licked.

She moaned.

He paused, taken aback. He'd never been with a moaner. His past girlfriends—the list was short, as he was a serial monogamist—had lain silent and so relaxed, they seemed to be sleeping.

He licked again, and Emma writhed. Encouraged, he licked and stroked and skimmed her folds with his tongue, each touch bringing from her another movement, another sound, another arch of the back.

She tasted like chocolate and a hint of salt. Her flesh was smooth and elastic, a complex puzzle of ridges and valleys. She had little hair compared to the other women he'd been with, and her sex was sweet and smooth against his mouth. Each of his touches made her mewl in pleasure; it made him want to lick her forever, his own sex responding to her reactions.

He found her opening with the tip of his tongue and pressed gently against it, seeking out her moisture.

Emma tensed, raising her hips against his mouth. His tongue was a taunt, promising what it could not deliver. Her whole body was poised to orgasm, but she wanted him deep inside her when she did. She wanted to feel herself filled; wanted him to thrust into her and stretch her to her limit.

"Now, now!" Emma said, reaching down and touching the sides of his head, gently urging him up. "Now, please!"

He rose up between her legs. She grabbed a pillow and arched her hips off the bed, shoving the pillow beneath her bottom, her hips now tilted for better G-spot stimulation, her thighs parted and her body waiting in wet hunger for him to enter. *Yes, yes, yes!* Finally!

She reached down and helped guide him to her entrance. He pressed into her and after a moment of blunt pressure she felt herself open to accept him, the hard width of him forcing its way inside. It was what she'd been yearning for in all her lonely nights, and the first moments were almost enough to send her over the edge.

He entered with short thrusts, going deeper into her each

time, her moisture easing his way. But as he stretched her, discomfort slipped in alongside her pleasure. It had been so long since she'd had sex, her body was no longer used to stretching to accept a man. But her body was still ready for pleasure; still seeking it; and she wrapped her legs around his waist and held on, urging him onward.

Supporting himself on his arms, he looked down at her as if asking for permission, his face tense with passion.

"Go for it," she whispered.

He went for it. He lowered himself to his forearms, holding her shoulders to keep her from being rocked against the brass bars of the headboard as he thrust like his life depended on it. She wrapped her arms around him and clawed gently at his back as he took her. His face was beside hers and she could hear and feel his breath near her ear. Sweat stuck their skin together, her thighs against his sides, his chest against her breasts.

The discomfort had lessened and she now felt nothing but the force of his passion; then thrust by thrust, the pleasure began to return. Just a tickle; a tease of excitement deep within her. A spot that his manhood stroked, bringing it slowly to life.

She clung to him more tightly and rocked her hips against him, trying to steal more of that faint pleasure. She tightened her inner muscles.

"Oh God, Emma," he said on a breath, his motions slowing, his whole body tensing.

No, not yet! she silently begged. Just when she was starting to enjoy it again!

One more thrust and then he was gripping her shoulders, and through the sensitive flesh at her entrance she felt the throb of his orgasm.

Dammit! Dammit dammit dammit!

He eased gently down on top of her, his body relaxing.

"It's okay, I can take your weight," she whispered, sensing that he was holding himself partly off her.

"Are you sure?"

She nodded, and was rewarded with his body heavy against her own. She closed her eyes, her arms still around him. She unwrapped her legs from his waist and lowered them, shaking with weariness, to the mattress. She gently stroked his back with her fingertips, as if soothing him to sleep.

"You didn't get your turn," he said.

It took her a moment to understand what he meant. "That's not what this is about. I'm here to please *you*."

He didn't answer, and she didn't know if he liked what she'd said or if it had reminded him too much of their arrangement.

"I'm crushing you," he said softly.

"No. I like it." She meant it, too. She liked the weight of him; liked being pinned beneath him, his member still embedded inside her. She felt vulnerable and protected all at once. It might not be an orgasm, but it gave her satisfaction to have him there.

They stayed that way for a short time longer and then he shifted, and they carefully disengaged their bodies. Emma cursed herself for having forgotten to have a towel ready, and grabbed the sheet from the bottom of the bed to put into makeshift use.

"You can take a shower if you'd like," she said.

He stood beside the bed, his staff still rigid. "I'll just clean myself up a bit," he said, and gathered his clothes, carrying them with him to the bathroom, his nakedness looking a bit awkward now; almost embarrassing, now that the passion had been spent.

Emma found her robe and threw it on, then started to clean up. The bowl of pudding went to the kitchen, the sheets were stripped, the candles were snuffed, the fishnets and maid's cap taken off. It would be more romantic to leave it all in place until he was gone, but her nervousness was returning. How did one say good night to one's lover/employer?

If he were her boyfriend he wouldn't be leaving at all, but would snuggle with her on the couch, eating ice cream and watching TV. He wouldn't be getting dressed and driving home, leaving her with dishes and laundry, an empty bed and a flush Visa card.

Russ used a washcloth to clean himself up and quickly got dressed in the bathroom. A glance in the mirror revealed mussed hair and a smear of pudding on his cheek. He washed it off and used wet hands to smooth his hair.

Emma's comb was on the counter, but to use it would be too intimate.

He breathed a laugh at that. Too intimate to use her comb without permission, after what they'd just done?

And yet it was true, and he dressed without using any of her things beyond the washcloth, which he tossed into her hamper. When he finished dressing he glanced around the small room, at the embroidered details on the shower curtain; at the porcelain toothbrush holder; at the framed series of small black-and-white photos of various foreign toilets. A bit of her humor there, he thought.

He glanced around once more, remembering the noises she had made before coming to the bedroom. What had she been doing? There was no clue to the mystery, and he couldn't ask her.

He left the bathroom and found her in the kitchen, wearing a silky floral robe and loading the dishwasher. The bright overhead light and the homely chore dispelled whatever lingering hint of romantic intimacy there might have been, and he felt he had overstayed himself already.

"I'll be going, then," he said, feeling exposed and vaguely ashamed of himself.

She straightened and turned around, holding a dirty dish in one hand and a too-cheerful smile on her lips. "Oh, okay! I hope that tonight . . . Well, you know. That it was what you were hoping for. Was it okay?"

Christ. She was asking for a performance evaluation.

"Everything was wonderful. You obviously put a lot of thought and hard work into it." He grimaced at his own words. "I mean, into the meal. Into the other bit as well." He snapped his lips shut before he could dig himself in any deeper.

"I'm glad you liked it. The meal, I mean. And the rest." She bit her lip, then her eyes widened. "Oh, I almost forgot!" She grabbed two plastic containers off the counter and thrust them at him. "Leftovers, if you want them."

"You don't?"

She shrugged. "I can cook. You can't. Besides, I still have the ice cream."

He accepted the containers. "Thanks. This should last me through the weekend."

"Good." She smiled, and a silent moment stretched between them. "I'll—" she started.

"I'll—" he said at the same time, and stopped. "You first."

"I was just going to say, 'I'll see you Monday, then?' Same time?"

"Yes."

"Great!"

They went to the door together and there was another moment of tense awkwardness. "Good night, then," he said.

"Yes, good night."

He opened the door and looked back at her, trying to read her expression. Trying to see if she wanted a good-night kiss, or if she just wanted him gone. He couldn't tell.

"Sleep well," he said, and then gestured to the containers. "And thanks."

"You're welcome. Drive safe."

"Good night."

" 'Night."

He turned and walked down the corridor, and heard her gently close the door to the apartment.

When he was back in his car and driving home, his brain began to torment him with self-doubt as he mentally replayed the events. He'd bored her at dinner; he'd been stiff and awkward in conversation and action; he hadn't given her an orgasm.

He felt the burn of embarrassment on his face. *He hadn't given her an orgasm.*

Maybe she hadn't enjoyed *any* of it. Maybe the moans and writhing had all been for show, to make him feel good about his prowess. He'd never been with a woman who made so much noise. "*I'm here to please you,*" she'd said. Maybe writhers and moaners existed only in the land of make-believe.

Ah, Christ. He'd just had the most surprising, most erotic, most weirdly exciting sex of his life, and all he could think was that she probably hadn't enjoyed a bit of it. She'd probably been imagining herself anywhere but in bed with him, her mind a thousand miles away. He may as well have been masturbating.

This was no way for a man with self-respect to entertain himself. He'd call her tomorrow and end it.

Seven

I can't believe you lucked into this place so fast," Daphne said, finding a spot on the windowsill for the plant she'd brought as a housewarming gift.

"God, I'm envious," Emma's friend Beth said, from the futon couch that was the only piece of furniture in the living area. "You're single, thin, and living in a posh apartment in Belltown."

"Don't give me that. I remember how loud and long you moaned about being single. You couldn't wait to get married and pregnant and move to the burbs."

Beth put her hands on her eighth-month belly and made a face. "That was before I knew what was in store for me, or that Ty was only pretending to know how to use a washing machine. Do you know, he leaves his dirty clothes all over the house. You'd think a grown man would know better than to take off clothes at random and drop them on the floor. I'm *pregnant*, for God's sake! Does he think it's easy for me to bend down and pick them up? It's frickin' impossible!"

"You'd better take her out to lunch," Daphne said in a stage whisper. "Blood sugar. Dangerously low."

"Just you wait," Beth said. "Derek will be just as bad. Oh, they pretend to cook for themselves and to keep their bathroom clean *before* you're legally bound to them, but the moment they've got you locked up in their pumpkin shell, there they keep you very well!" She angrily plucked at the fringe on the pillow.

"What happened to the glow of pregnancy?" Emma asked.

"Fuck the glow! It's a fucking lie!" Beth started to cry.

Emma and Daphne exchanged wide-eyed glances; then both went to sit on either side of Beth and comfort her.

"It's nothing like I thought it would be," Beth said, wiping at her running nose with the back of her hand and snuffling. "Everything on TV makes it look so *lovely* and *beautiful* and like it's going to be the best thing in the world. They don't tell you what's going to happen to your body. They don't tell you that you can hardly breathe, or sleep at night, or that you have to pee every ten minutes. They don't tell you that you can't stay awake for more than a few hours, or that your emotions get all wonky so that you start crying for no flippin' reason. They don't tell you that you'll be frickin' *scared to death* about everything that could go wrong, and that your husband will just say, 'You worry too much. Women drop babies in rice paddies in China all the time and just keep on working, no problem. You'll be fine.' I'm not a fucking farmer in a rice paddy! I'll bet they're just as pissed off at their husbands, anyway! Who leaves a woman to give birth in a rice paddy?"

Beth snuffled. "I haven't even chosen a theme yet for the baby's room. What type of mother am I?"

Emma wrapped her arms around her and gave her a hug. "Maybe a normal one."

Beth sniffled. "You think so?"

Daphne's cell phone rang, playing a snippet of The Rolling Stones's "You Can't Always Get What You Want." "Hi, sweetie! Yeah, I'm about done here . . ." Her voice faded out as she went into the other room to finish her conversation.

"Are things really so bad?" Emma asked Beth.

Beth shrugged. "I don't know. I can't tell anymore. It's like I have the worst case of PMS ever, times ten. It messes up my perspective, but I swear, Ty doesn't understand anything about what I'm going through."

"Ty adores you."

"I think he's afraid of me." Beth smiled through her tears. "For good reason, maybe. The happy woman he married has turned into a lunatic." Her smile faded. "And the tender, affectionate man I married has turned into someone who plays deaf if I try to talk during a 'big moment' in a ball game on TV."

"Oh."

"Yeah. I make him pay for that, though," Beth said darkly.

Daphne emerged from the other room. "I gotta run. I'm meeting Derek at his house and then we're going furniture shopping. Woo hoo! He knows I hate his black leather sofa, and I love how he's making compromises for me."

"It's sounding pretty serious," Emma said. "How much have you guys been talking about the future?"

Daphne's grin wavered only the faintest bit. "Oh, it's too soon to get into that."

Emma and Beth exchanged a quick, silent look, but Daphne caught it. "What?! I'm not going to rush him! I don't want to scare him off. This is a big step as it is, moving in together."

"Just as long as you're both on the same page about what you want for the future," Emma said.

Beth added, "You've talked about whether he'd like to be married eventually and have kids, haven't you?"

"It's too soon!" Daphne insisted. "Asking me to live with him is a huge step, and I don't think he would have taken it if he didn't see a future for us."

Emma put up her hands in surrender. "Okay, okay, you know him a lot better than either of us do. I'll be here if you need me, but I know you're confident you won't."

"Thanks for the thought." Daphne came over to give Emma a hug. "I'm going to miss living with you. You'll come over to our place for dinner sometime, won't you?"

"Sure. And you can come down here and we'll go shopping and have lunch."

"Okay."

Daphne said her good-byes to Beth and then left.

"I hope that works out as well as she hopes," Beth said.

"Daphne and Derek?" At Beth's nod Emma shrugged. "I guess I hope so, too."

"You don't like Derek?"

"I don't know. There's nothing wrong with him, really, except that he strikes me as kind of dim. No imagination. But maybe Daphne doesn't mind that."

"Who can tell what type of partner is right for someone else? We can't even judge that for ourselves. Speaking of which! What's the full story on this apartment and the guy who owns it, huh?"

Emma felt her cheeks redden. "Why should my getting this apartment have anything to do with romance?"

Beth raised a brow. "No way you can afford this place on your own. Belltown is *muy* trendy, and trendy means bucks. So come on, spill! Or better yet, let's go have lunch and then you can spill over the food. I'm *starving!* But let me go to the bathroom first."

There was no shortage of restaurants in Belltown, and the apartment was within walking distance of both tourist-choked Pike Place Market and the main shopping district in the center of the city, home to upscale malls, department stores, and boutiques. They decided on a bistro a block and a half from the apartment and settled into a booth by the window, where the spring sunlight could warm their skin.

Two baskets full of bread, a bowl of lobster bisque, and another bathroom trip later, Beth put down her spoon and sighed. "Ohhh, that's better."

"You're not going to have room for your entrée."

"Ha—watch me. But now, tell me what's up with the apartment."

Emma played with the remains of her salad, driving a candied pecan through an oil slick of balsamic vinaigrette. For the past twenty minutes she'd been debating how much to tell Beth, trying to guess her reaction if she heard the whole truth.

"Like I said, the apartment belongs to a rich man whose house I was cleaning. It's been empty for a few months; he hasn't had time to find a tenant and he thinks he wants to sell the place soon, so he's letting me stay there for a very reasonable price."

Beth gnawed a crust of bread. "Mm-hm. And is he single?"

"Well, yeah," Emma conceded.

"How old?"

Emma shifted in her seat. "Thirty-six."

"Good-looking?"

"Maybe."

"Uh-huh. I see."

Emma met her eyes, trying to keep hers innocent. "You see what?"

"Has he made a pass at you?"

"Maybe." A smile pulled at the corner of her mouth. "And it's not like I haven't wanted to lay my hands on *his* fine ass."

"Emma!"

"What?!"

"Naughty girl." Beth grinned. "You want him, don't you?"

Emma shrugged.

"He must want you, too. Why else would he let you have the apartment? I bet he's going to make excuses to stop by and 'see how you're doing.' He'll bring instructions to the microwave or pretend there's a leak in the bathroom faucet."

"He hardly needs to make excuses. I offered to make him dinner whenever he wants."

"Emma!"

"There's nothing wrong with making him dinner."

"Of course there's not. I'm just surprised. I've never known you to make a move on a guy."

"They say the way to a man's heart is through his stomach." Emma grinned.

Beth snorted. "I think there's another organ that takes priority. But you're a fabulous cook, and men love food. Have you ever thought about going into catering?"

"No," she said, glad to change the topic. "Being a personal chef crossed my mind, but I'm not going to pursue it for fear of getting sidetracked from architecture." A faint thought flitted through her mind, a distant sense that the pieces of her puzzle had not been put together correctly. She'd offered to cook for Russ the first time she met him . . .

"Makes sense, I guess," Beth said. "But back to your love slave: I never knew you were attracted to older guys."

The thought Emma had been trying to capture dissipated as she switched her attention to Beth's comment. "He doesn't seem older, except that he doesn't walk around with a baseball cap on sideways, doesn't wear a gold chain around his neck, and I can't imagine him sitting around with his buddies drinking beer and talking about how 'hot' some girl is."

"Since when do guys grow out of that?"

Emma shrugged. "He just doesn't seem that way. He drives a hybrid, for God's sake. Granted, a Lexus high-performance hybrid, but still a hybrid."

"That means nothing. Hybrids are status symbols now: they say, "I'm smart enough to care about the environment, and rich enough to act on it." And a Lexus performance car *screams,* 'I have money. Fuck me!' Granted, it screams it in a more gentlemanly manner than a Porsche, but it's the same thing."

"So what if he *is* looking for sex? It's not like I don't want that myself."

"But you don't want to be his young little sex trophy, either, stashed away in his apartment to come pork whenever he feels like it."

Emma scowled. "Why not? Why not for once just have

fun with sex, instead of trying to tie it up into a big compli-
cated relationship? I don't have *time* for a relationship. I
don't feel like nurturing some guy's ego and having him
suck up all my free time. I have better things to do!"

Beth gaped at her.

The waitress set their lunches in front of them. "Is there
anything else I can bring you?"

Emma flashed her a smile. "No, thanks."

The aroma of chicken cacciatore stirred Beth back to the
present. "I always thought it was true love and Prince
Charming you were waiting for. I never thought you cared
about sex for the sake of sex."

Emma dug into her grilled salmon. "Yeah, well. Just because I didn't have any for a long time doesn't mean I didn't
want it."

"But do you really not care about not having a relationship along with it?"

"I just . . ." she started, but then couldn't find words to
explain what she had not yet completely reconciled within
herself. "I just know that I'm horny and that I want to devote my energies to my career right now. Can I have sex on
a regular basis with the same man and not get emotionally
involved? I don't know. I've never tried."

"Can you even enjoy it that way?"

"I'm willing to give it a shot."

"I had a few relationships like that, where by the end I
didn't care about the guy," Beth said. "Whenever we had sex,

while I was lying under him and he was grunting away on me, tears would roll down my cheeks. The worst part of it was that the jerk never even noticed."

"Jeez, Beth. If you were crying during sex, why did you keep doing it?"

She shrugged. "The relationships usually ended a couple weeks later. It became a pretty good warning sign that things had gone sour."

"I should think so."

"The weird thing was, I didn't know that I felt nothing for the guy anymore until I started crying. It's like my body knew, even if my brain didn't."

Emma shivered. "I hope that doesn't happen to me."

"If it does, don't ignore it. No orgasm is worth feeling like crap."

Emma tried to shake Beth's words off. "I wonder if men ever feel that way?"

"I can't imagine that they do. An orgasm is an orgasm is an orgasm to them. What's not to like? I mean, they pay hookers for sex, and that's got to be about as 'I don't care about her' as you can get."

"I guess you're right," Emma said weakly.

"Isn't there a famous quote that goes something like, 'Men don't pay women for sex. They pay them to go away after.' "

Emma was getting queasy. She wanted Russ to like her; to respect her, even. To enjoy spending time with her. "I read somewhere that when a man comes, he gets the same burst of oxytocin that a woman gets when someone hugs her."

"What's oxytocin?" Beth asked.

"You know, it's that hormone that makes people bond to each other. Mothers to babies, women to men. You'll supposedly get big bursts of it when you breast-feed."

"God, I hope so. At the moment I feel like this baby is the alien that took over my body."

"Anyway, women get bursts of oxytocin when they're touched. Men only get a healthy dose of it when they come. It makes them feel love. Supposedly." Emma shrugged.

"Which would explain why they declare their devotion after they've had their little 'moment.' And here I always thought it was gratitude for sex that prompted that 'I love you.'"

Emma laughed. "Nope. Chemicals."

Beth sighed. "I always knew that I'd better put out on a regular basis if I didn't want Ty to stray."

"I hope there's more to his fidelity than that," Emma said. "I hope there's more to *any* guy's fidelity. We can't all be the same to them."

Beth speared a mushroom with her fork. "Just a hole to put it in. That's all we are."

"You don't really believe that, do you?"

"I don't know. Sometimes I feel like all I am to Ty is that woman who does his laundry and cooks his dinner, and who's convenient when he wants to get off. He doesn't even seem interested in the baby." Beth sniffled.

"But you know he loves you."

"Does he? Maybe it's the path of least resistance for him to stay with me. He hates confrontation. He'd rather endure misery in silence than fight."

"But I think that's true of most guys," Emma protested. "Have you talked to him? Let him know how you're feeling?"

Beth snorted. "Oh, yeah, that will go over well. The last thing a guy wants to hear from any woman is, 'We need to talk.' No, I think your plan to seduce your cute landlord is better than I first thought: sex without attachment, where you can take what you need and leave the rest of the relationship mess behind. Everything will be on your own terms."

"That's what I'm hoping," Emma said, but found herself plagued by a niggling sense of doubt.

Eight

W hat's all this?" Russ asked.

Emma looked up from where she was pouring the juices out of the roasting pan into a small bowl. "Don't look at those!" How could she have forgotten to hide her dismal sketches for the train station?

"What are they?" he asked again, a glass of Chianti in one hand, the other hand moving the sketches around her drafting table.

Emma slammed down the pan and scampered around the breakfast bar to the living room. "Don't look! They're terrible!" She grabbed the papers and flipped them over.

"I didn't see anything terrible. What are they drawings of?"

"They're designs for a train station," she admitted. "For the King Street Station, actually. There's a contest."

"That's right, I heard about that. So you're going to enter?"

"Not if I can't think up anything better than this," she said.

"If I can offer a piece of advice?"

She stiffened, wary of criticism. "What?"

"I don't know anything about architecture, but I know a little about committees. Whatever key words or phrases they use in describing the objective of the contest, be sure to repeat those same words and phrases back to them in the description of your entry. They love that."

"Oh," she said, and blinked in surprise. "That's very helpful."

He laughed. "You didn't think I was going to try to give you advice on the design, did you?" He gestured at the photos on the wall. "With an eye like yours, I have no doubt you'll come up with something stunning."

She smiled crookedly. "Thanks for the confidence. I wish I shared it."

"If you keep working at it, I'm sure you'll surprise yourself with what you can create."

Emma headed back to the kitchen, hoping that was true. Everything she drew felt hopelessly pedestrian. No hint of flair, no nod to the uniqueness of Seattle beyond the tired attempt to throw salmon and fir trees into the design.

Over the weekend she'd found herself abandoning her drawings in favor of preparing for tonight; it was more entertaining to plan a complex dinner and sexual escapade than to sit and stare at blank paper and face the fear that she didn't possess the creativity she needed.

Tonight's sexual extravagance was number 64 from *101 Ways to Shock His Rocks,* a piece of fine literature she'd purchased at a sex shop. Personally, she thought that number 64 was treading into disturbing territory, but the description promised to draw a night of unforgettable, primitive passion from her man. Who was she to argue? She'd thought that most of the stuff in the sex shop was icky, but it wouldn't be such a profitable business if it didn't deliver what it promised.

At least, that's what she'd told herself as she handed her Visa to the cashier and slunk out of the store with a big plastic bag of obscene treasures.

She plated their meals and carried them and the bowl of pan juices out to the table. Russ joined her.

"Duck stuffed with chicken liver, candied orange, and pears," she announced, setting the plates down. "Green beans braised with tomatoes and basil. And there's a cream cheese *crostata* with orange marmalade for dessert."

"This is amazing."

She stared at the plates of food, so prettily done, and frowned. "It's not."

"What?"

She sat down as he held her chair for her and clenched her teeth against the threat of tears. "It's just recipes from a magazine. I didn't even come up with menu myself: I used the magazine for that, too."

"Uh . . . so?"

She shook her head angrily. "No creativity! A true cook creates her own recipes and instinctively understands what foods go together to make a meal. I just follow the directions I'm given!"

"I'd have a mess on my hands if I tried that. I probably wouldn't know what half the ingredients were, to begin with."

"But maybe you'd be creative. I'm not—I don't take any risks. I don't substitute, I don't experiment, or vary. I don't fling things together with whatever is in the pantry."

He was quiet, seeming not to know how to respond. Why was she dumping this on him? He wasn't her boyfriend. He wasn't here to listen to her problems; he was here for a pleasant evening of food and sex.

"Let's eat," she said, picking up her fork. "It's getting cold."

They ate in silence for several minutes. Emma stewed in a broth of her own insecurities, basting herself with self-criticism. When Russ spoke, it was as if the words were coming from far away and it took her a moment to hear what he was asking.

"Did your mother cook this way? Duck, chicken livers, etcetera."

"Sometimes. Not usually. It would be a bit much for two picky kids."

"So once you were on your own, you started cooking this way?"

She laughed. "It's not exactly in my budget."

"And yet you expect yourself to have mastery of a skill that people spend a lifetime developing?"

She stabbed a bean with her fork and lifted it up as Exhibit A. "Beans and tomatoes are humble ingredients. There should be creativity even with humble ingredients. I've cooked plenty of beans and tomatoes in my life. Why did I never think to put them together?"

"That's an impossible question. You may as well ask why you never paired beans with apricots or peanuts or kumquats."

"I appreciate your attempt at logic." She knew he was trying to help, but sometimes logic didn't tell the whole story. "The answer would be the same, though: I'm not a creative cook."

"You're too hard on yourself. It takes mastery of the basics of any skill before creativity and experimentation can be done with a regular degree of success. I doubt that at your age you have sufficient mastery of any skill to allow you to be a creative genius in its sphere."

"I think you meant to comfort me by saying that," Emma commented wryly.

A little frown of worry appeared between his brows. "Did I succeed?"

She shrugged one shoulder, feeling a bit better despite herself. "Perhaps."

He nodded in satisfaction and turned his attention to the duck, cutting off a neat piece with knife and fork. "Good. A bit of reason is more effective than a hug. Lasts longer, too."

Emma coughed on her sip of wine. "I'm no longer puzzled that you're not married yet."

He looked at her in surprise.

"Oh, come on," she said. "Don't tell me you honestly don't see that a woman you were romantically involved with would want the hug first, reasoning later. If at all."

"But reasoning and thoughts do affect a person's emotional state."

"And so does a hug, at least for a woman. And the hug will get quicker results."

"Give a woman a hug and she's happy for a day. Teach a woman to reason and—"

"You did *not* just say that."

"No, I didn't. You interrupted me."

She raised one brow. "Excuse me. You were saying?"

"Teach a woman to reason, and she'll find seventeen ways in which you are wrong, with subparts A and B for six of them."

"You have a hostile view toward women, don't you? I thought you were just kidding, that first day when you told Kevin that gold diggers would be after him."

"It's not a hostile view."

"Then what is it?"

He chewed for a minute, then glanced her way. "Wary."

She cocked her head. "Wary? Why?"

"Alien race. Can't predict what they're going to do. How they're going to react."

Had someone hurt him, beyond the ordinary heartbreaks of love? Emma stared at him, trying to discern the truth from the subtle clues hidden in inflections of his voice and the microexpressions of his face.

"Men and women hurt each other," she said. "That's never going to change; it comes with the territory. But it's a glorious territory, all considered, and I wouldn't want to live my life without spending a good deal of time in it."

"Just not now."

"No, not at this moment. Except like this," she said, gesturing between them. She looked at him for a moment, considering. "Can I tell you something?"

"Sure."

"I wasn't certain, initially, that I wanted to do this. I mean, it's kind of sleazy-sounding on the surface, don't you think? After all, being paid for sex isn't exactly what most girls aim for in life."

"Er, no, I suppose not."

"But the truth is," she said, leaning forward confidentially, "I'm kind of having fun."

His brows rose.

"I know! It's crazy, isn't it? And the naughtiness kind of turns me on. I know that submitting to a man's sexual appetites for the sake of money is supposed to be degrading. I'm supposed to be ashamed. But I'm not. Bad me, huh? And bad, wicked you."

"I've thought a hundred times about canceling our arrangement."

That surprised her.

He went on, "You're not the only one who feels they're supposed to hold themselves to a higher standard of behavior."

"Then why didn't you call this off?"

He looked at her incredulously. "You really need to ask?"

A slow grin stretched across her lips. "You like it, don't you?"

"Don't look at me like that."

"Like what?"

"Like a witch who has her victim under her spell."

"Is that what I've done? Ensorcelled you?"

Emma felt a surge of arousal. She would never have guessed that a man could want her badly enough that he would go against his own sense of decency to have her. No one had *ever* wanted her like that.

She stood and came around the small table to him, feeling utterly confident. She slid her hand around his neck and kissed him slowly, brushing him gently at first and then running her tongue lightly over his bottom lip.

He turned toward her, hands going to her waist, his desire answering her demands. Without thinking she straddled him, sitting on his lap with her panty-clad crotch wide open and pressed against the zipper of his trousers. She felt him thickening beneath her, and rubbed herself against him.

The kiss deepened, mouths opening, and she sucked on

his tongue, sliding her own along it, reveling in the texture and the memory of what that tongue had done to her before. She felt his hand in her hair, holding her to him as if he would devour her. The strength of his arm around her waist felt better than anything else, the power of his lust and of his male body, so much larger than hers, making her feel deliciously small and desirable. She'd brought him to this state of arousal, and now she wanted him to set her free of control. She wanted to be taken.

Which reminded her. "We still have *crostata* to eat," she breathed, breaking the kiss.

"Forget the *crostata*."

She found purchase on the floor for her feet and lifted her weight off his lap. After a moment his arms around her loosened and she climbed off him, going back to her place at the table. She picked up her flatware as if to resume eating.

"*Crostata?*" he said in disbelief.

She looked at him and smiled with satisfaction. His shirt and hair were rumpled and he looked like someone had just woken him from a dream. "I worked very hard on it. I also worked hard on my preparations for the other things we're going to do tonight."

"Flexibility in the face of changing circumstances is very good for creativity," he said earnestly.

She laughed. "Maybe. But you still have to wait."

Emma cut herself another bite of duck and felt a quiver

of doubt. Maybe it wasn't so wise to stop now. Maybe it would be better to go for it while the mood was upon them, instead of trying to make the evening fit her carefully planned script.

But after all that planning and practicing and debating and buying the right music, she couldn't bring herself to alter her plan.

She ate the last of her duck, which had turned out better than any duckly improvisation she could have made. Maybe Russ was right, and she shouldn't expect herself, with her limited experience, to be able to innovate.

But then where did that leave her chances with designing the train station? Maybe she was reaching beyond her grasp.

The small voice of her soul rebelled against the thought, just as it had always rebelled—quietly, often unobserved—when she felt that someone expected less of her than she expected of herself. She never wanted to be mediocre or settle for "good enough." It was the curse of being a perfectionist.

There must have been a hard-driven perfectionist inside of Russ, as well, to have achieved what he had. How else was a young person going to make it in this world?

"These are your instructions."

Russ took the typed sheet that Emma handed him. "Instructions?"

"For our 'entertainment' tonight."

Instructions. Great. He scanned the sheet, his attention

catching at the script in the middle. "You want me to say that?" he asked in disbelief.

She nodded, her face serious. "Please."

He scanned the rest of the sheet, growing alarmed. "You're sure about this?"

She nodded.

"I don't want you to get hurt."

"I won't. And look, see there?" She reached over the top of the paper and pointed to one short sentence. "That's our 'safe' word: *apple*. If I say *apple*, then we stop."

Hell's bells. He'd never engaged in sexual activities that required a safe word. It was on the tip of his tongue to ask her to forget this crazy plan and just have good, plain, old-fashioned sex. But then he met her eyes and saw the uncertain, hopeful expectation there, and he remembered that she'd worked so hard on her plans for this evening. "Okay, let's give this a go."

She smiled and turned him toward her bedroom, giving him a small shove. "You go lounge on the bed while I get ready. And there's something there for you to put on."

Oh Lord. He could hardly wait to see.

The bedroom was again lit softly with candles, and this time the bed had been turned into the divan of a pasha. Jewel-toned fabrics with gold prints covered the mattress, the pillows, and lumps that were probably heaped blankets serving as the arms and back of the exotic love nest. In the center of a swath of royal blue fabric sat a red satin turban, complete with fake diamond in the front, a small gold feather sticking straight up from behind it. It looked like the turban that Johnny Carson wore whenever he played Karnak the Magnificent.

Russ sighed and glanced again at his instruction sheet:

You are the sultan of a small country on the Mediterranean, and have bought a young English noblewoman from pirates. Your other concubines have been training her for your service, and tonight is the first night you will have her. When the eunuchs deliver her to your room, follow the script below.

He lifted the turban and went to the mirror, where he settled the turban onto his head. It was heavy, straining his neck with the effort of keeping his head up when there was the least hint of imbalance.

He looked like a clown. She couldn't possibly find this sexy.

With a shake of his head he went to the bed/divan and tried to make himself comfortable, spreading his arms out over the "back" and stretching his legs out in front of him, crossed at the ankles.

The turban pulled his head back, and he let it go until a pillow bumped up against the back, shoving it forward and down lower over his brows, but also helping to support it.

He just knew that self-consciousness was going to prevent him from performing sexually. There was no way he could get aroused while dressed like this, speaking those words on the paper.

He closed his eyes and tried to ignore his surroundings, picturing how Emma had looked when she opened the door to him this evening, her hair done up loosely with tendrils hanging down, her tight light green T-shirt showing the outline of her bra and clinging faithfully to her shape. She was wearing a short pleated skirt that had offered no resistance when she straddled him during dinner.

He felt a faint tingle of life in his loins.

A strain of music drifted to him from the living room, and he almost recognized it. A few bars later he had it: "The Young Prince and Princess" from Rimsky-Korsakov's *Scheherazade*.

The tingle of life died away, as he was reminded of this harem scene in which he had to play his ridiculous role.

"Unhand me, you filthy cad!" Emma shrieked in a fake English accent that sounded more like Cockney Eliza Doolittle than a gently bred young lady.

He opened his eyes just as she threw herself into the bedroom, landing on all fours in front of the bed. For a moment he thought she had dumped a basket of laundry over herself, but then she raised her head and he saw that she had a scarf covering her face except for her eyes, her dark hair spilling in disarray around her shoulders. The rest of her getup came into focus: a dark pink bra-and-panty set with a dozen silk scarves attached all around, both top and bottom.

She turned and looked back over her shoulder, addressing her imaginary captors. "Ye brutes! When me faither gits ahold o'ye, ye'll be paying with yer hides! Ye'll not fergit that it was Lord Oakley's daughter that ye did this to."

She turned to him and narrowed her eyes, slowly rising from the floor until she stood before him, her chin raised in defiance. "Ye'll not be taming me, sirrah!"

He gaped at her.

She scowled and nodded strangely with her head. "Sirrah! Ye'll not be taming me!"

"Oh! Oh, sorry!" He grabbed the paper and scanned down to the script. "You'll part your thighs for me, wench, and you'll like it," he read stiffly.

"Never! Ye shall never sully the rose o'me virginity, ye scurvy dog!" She lowered her voice to a stage whisper. "Put some emotion into it, Russ!"

He cleared his throat and lowered his voice. "Your rose is mine to pluck, saucy wench."

She put her hand on her hip and tossed her head. "It'll be me thorns yer tastin', not me precious petals."

"You're mine now, and the sooner you submit to me, the happier you'll be."

"Never! I'll die first!"

There was a line of stage direction. He paused to read it, then declared, "First, you'll dance!" He clapped his hands in the air. "Dance for me, wench, as my concubines have trained you!" He clapped again. "Dance!"

"I will not!"

"Dance, or I'll give you a taste of the bastinado. You'll not like to have the soles of your feet beaten, my comely wench. Dance! Or feel my wrath."

"You would beat me?"

"Disobey me once more, and you will feel the cruelty of my anger. Dance!"

She put her hands over her veiled face and pretended to sob.

"And call me 'Master,' " Russ threw in for the hell of it.

She peeped over her fingers, a questioning look in her eyes.

"Why do you stand there, wench?" he ad-libbed, abandoning sanity and going with the absurd drama Emma seemed so determined to play out. "Dance!"

"Yes, Master," she said, and dropped her hands, her gaze fixing on the floor as if in shameful submission.

The Rimsky-Korsakov piece had just started to repeat itself. Emma swayed gently to it, the scarves—veils, he supposed she meant them to be—following her movements and reminding him of the floppy rags that shook themselves over your vehicle while going through a car wash.

She lifted her arms and rose up onto her toes, still swaying, and started to move around the room in some perversion of ballet moves, from the looks of it. His momentary amusement began to fade and a faint embarrassment crept in. She wasn't a particularly graceful dancer, nor an erotic one, and his imagination simply couldn't transform her panty set and scarves into a harem girl's sultry silks.

She pranced in a circle, then stopped in front of him and seesawed her hips up and down. She snaked her arms in the air and moved her torso in an undulation that looked like nothing so much as a boa constrictor swallowing a large animal. Good God, had she made this up herself, or had she paid someone to teach her to do this?

He was gathering courage to tell her that Master wanted something different, when she plucked the first scarf off her costume and let it flutter to the floor. It revealed one cup of the bra—which had slits down the center of the cups, allowing the nipple to poke through.

His gaze attached to that revealed nipple, pinched in the slit of dark pink fabric, and he forgot about asking her to stop.

Another veil fell to the floor, revealing a length of thigh. A curve of back appeared. A buttock. She danced between each revelation, her movements seeming saucy taunts now, teasing him, prolonging the unveiling of her lithe body. Soon she was wearing nothing but her undergarments, the veil over her face, and one scarf tucked into the top of her panties, hanging down over her loins. His gaze flitted back and forth between her nipples and that last piece of filmy fabric, unable to decide which was more enticing.

At last she plucked the final veil from her panties and let it fall to the floor. There was a tiny bow down low on her mound, and he realized that they were split-crotch panties. One tug on the end of the bow and they would open wide. Her hand brushed down over her panties and he held his breath, waiting for her to untie them.

Her hand moved away, leaving the bow still tied.

He was hard and ready, and the bow was now a fixation. He wanted her to untie it. Wanted her to part the lacy fabric and straddle him, lowering herself onto him and riding for all she was worth. He wanted to suck on her nipples, lapping at them through their slits, and have her arch her back and moan.

Instead, her dancing slowly stopped and her hands fell to her sides. She looked at the floor. " 'Tis all I know, Master."

She couldn't stop *now*! "Untie the bow. Now."

She slowly reached for it, grasping one end. She began to pull, the loop of bow shrinking. When it was almost at the point of release she stopped, her hand falling away. She turned her hips slightly away from him, as if in modesty. "I cannot! I will not shame meself!"

What was he supposed to do now? He snatched up the script and scanned down. Where were they? Ah, here it was. He read through the remainder of her instructions and just as when he'd first read the script, doubt assailed him.

He looked up and met her eyes. She was watching him, waiting. He raised his brows in question. Barely perceptible nodding was her answer, and he thought he saw the shadow of a smile beneath the veil over her face.

It wasn't his type of thing, but for her sake he'd go through the motions. He was going to feel like a fool, and already felt his excitement dying.

He put the paper aside and cleared his throat. "I told you, wench, that you'll not disobey me. Untie that bow!"

"No, sirrah!"

"That's 'Master' to you, wench."

"You'll never be my master!"

Oh, Lord. He really wasn't enjoying this. "Come here." She inched closer to him, standing a foot away.

"Closer."

She took a small step forward.

He reached out and tugged at the end of the bow. She stood motionless, letting him. It came undone and he pulled the ribbon completely free of the lace. He dropped it and brushed his fingertips lightly over her lace-clad mound. He could feel the damp heat of her exertions. He brushed over her again, feeling for the edges of the lace.

He glanced up at her. "Part your thighs."

She hesitated, then moved her feet apart a few scant inches, just enough so that he could slide two upturned fingers between her legs. She rocked forward against his hand, her breath catching. He found the center of her heat and gently pressed upward, teasing his fingertips back and forth to part the lace. It opened and one fingertip slipped in, stroking against her entrance, the pad of his finger barely parting her.

He could hear her breathing, and her excitement revived his own. He gently massaged his palm over her mound, his fingertip still against her opening, and felt her hips move in response. She made a soft noise deep in her throat and then pushed away from him, scampering several feet away.

He pushed up off the bed, grabbing the turban to keep it from falling off, and went after her, as her written instructions had dictated. She dashed away, his fingertips grazing her bare side as she exited the room.

He caught her in the living room, arms coming around her soft waist from behind. She held still for a moment, her breathing rapid, and let him slide his hand up her rib cage to one breast, where he gently pinched her nipple between his fingertips. His other hand slid downward to cup her sex. She leaned back against him, tilting her hips against his hand. He reached inside the slit of her bra and stroked the tender skin of her breast, then pulled down the strap that held it up, baring her breast entirely.

She pulled away from him again, dashing across the small room, freeing her arm from the trapping strap. She turned around and faced him, one breast bare, then feinted to one side. He went that way, and she switched directions. He let her go by, putting his hand out to brush along her as she passed by and scampered toward the bathroom.

He pursued, grabbing her around the waist before she

could reach its sanctuary. She twisted around in his arms and pushed against his chest in a mock struggle to get away. He held her more tightly, one hand going down to cup her buttock and pull her against him. With his other hand he pulled down the remaining strap, then reached behind her and unhooked her bra. It fell free, falling off her arm. She leaned away from him, arching her back, and he saw that the pale skin of her breasts was marked in pink vertical slashes where the lace slits had pressed against her skin. He lowered his mouth to one breast and laved tenderly at its silky surface. She struggled and raised her knee beside his hip as if trying to climb out of his grasp, in the process giving him access to her from below. His fingertips found her dampness, slipping between the strips of lace. This time he plunged an inch of finger inside her.

She went rigid, the hands that had been pushing him now clenching tight in the fabric of his shirt. She raised her veiled face, her dark eyes wide as they sought out his own. He looked into her eyes as he gently thrust his fingertip inside her, in and out, never more than an inch deep. He could feel her heart beating rapidly and watched as her eyes slowly closed. He felt his own arousal building, the exertion of the chase intensifying it.

She released his shirt and, fists clenched hard, shoved him firmly away. They struggled for a moment, but her efforts were harder this time and fear of hurting her made him let her escape.

She darted into the bedroom and started to close the door. He got himself in the path of the door before she could, his turban getting knocked off in the process and thumping to the floor behind him. He reached for her and she dashed away, picking up a scarf from the floor and throwing it at him.

He caught it and advanced on her, both of them breathing heavily now. With her veil, she was almost a creature unknown; a woman he'd never met. With her breasts bare beneath the hem of the veil and that hint of panty her only garb, she was a temptation he had no reason to resist. He'd become absorbed in the game, the primal instinct to hunt and capture fully aroused. Conscious thought was all but erased, the silk scarf in his hand the only reminder of what he must do before he could penetrate her.

Emma felt a flush of adrenaline as Russ stalked her, the silk scarf in his hands. Something near panic rushed in her blood and she felt the instinct to flee—the reflex of the hunted. She knew it would take but a single word to make him stop, but there was something delicious to being chased. She *wanted* to be frightened, overpowered, and taken, all within the safety of this play they had constructed.

He moved toward her, the intensity of his expression that of a wolf cornering prey. She gasped and darted past him. His arm caught her around the waist and swung her around, lifting her off her feet. She struggled within his grasp, the strength with which he held her sending bolts of alarm through her muscles. He was so much stronger than her, she couldn't break free unless he allowed it.

The security of his grip pushed her panic too close to the edge and she struggled harder, elbowing him. He released her and she darted from the room. She stood in the hall, panting, poised for further flight, waiting for him to chase after her and scared that he would. It took a moment for it to sink in that he *had* released her.

When he still didn't emerge from the doorway she crept back toward it, moving silently on the balls of her bare feet. She couldn't see him in the room, and couldn't hear him above the music and her own heavy breathing. She crept closer, leaning forward to peer into the room.

Still no sign of him.

She looked over her shoulder, suddenly certain he'd gotten behind her. As she did, her wrist was grabbed and she shrieked in surprise. He tugged her into the bedroom, and before she knew what he was doing he had bound her wrists together with the scarf. She made a token tug of resistance, and he scooped her up into his arms and carried her to the bed. He dropped her onto the pillows and put his hands to work on his belt buckle.

Emma flipped onto her stomach and crawled toward the far corner of the bed, over the mounds of blankets and pillows. She felt his hand on her ankle, pulling her slowly back toward the edge. She reached forward with her bound

140

hands, trying to find something to grab to slow her slide, but the brass bars of the bed were beyond reach.

He pulled until her legs were half off the bed, and with a few quick tugs he stripped her panties off her. Emma lay still, her cheek against the mattress, her arms stretched out in front of her. Her hair obscured her vision, and all she could see were shadows in the candlelight and the pillows near her.

His hands slid up the backs of her thighs, then up over the mounds of her buttocks. His palms explored her lower back, her hips, the place where her buttocks met her thighs. He brushed his hands along the insides of her thighs, rising up to but not quite touching her sex. He pulled her farther over the edge of the bed, until she had to bend her knees to keep from being unbalanced. The edge of the bed hit her at midthigh now.

She felt him gently parting her legs and obeyed the silent command. Cool air touched her most intimate area and then she felt his hands against her pushing to the sides, causing her flower to unfold and her entrance to part its lips. She closed her eyes, embarrassed, and tucked her nose and chin into the side of her arm.

He released her flesh and a moment later his hands were on her hips, urging her upward. He helped her onto her knees with her legs together, her forearms still on the mattress. She felt the blunt head of his rod against her opening, rubbing back and forth, its path becoming slippery with her moisture. He parted her thighs slightly and slid himself along the folds of her damp sex. His hips came up against her buttocks and he reached around to her front, his hand pressing downward on her mound as he slowly thrust between her slick folds.

She moaned deep in her throat as each thrust brought his head into contact with the nub of her pleasure. She rocked against him, joining his rhythm. His other hand cupped her breast, massaging it.

He pulled away, then pushed a big pillow under her and had her lie down on top of it, her hips raised up. Then he was parting her thighs and she felt him slowly enter her, thrusting in gradual, deepening strokes. Taking her without words, as if they were strangers.

When he'd made it halfway in he leaned forward, bracing himself on his rigid arms. She could feel the tension in him as he breathed her name and slowly thrust the rest of the way, embedding himself deep within her.

Emma instinctively wrapped her lower legs behind his back, her feet touching each other as she pulled him more securely to her.

"*Emma,*" he breathed again, and began to thrust, his angle bringing his rod in contact with that one sensitive spot inside her passage. She mewled in her throat and tried to move with him, but it was nearly impossible. She could only grip him with her legs and let him take her as he would.

For the first time in her life, she felt an orgasm approaching from penetration alone. She dug her fingernails into the silks, her body clenching and urging the passion upward. She squeezed her inner muscles, wanting to grasp all of him that she could, and a second later felt him slow.

"Oh God, Emma," he said, and grabbed her hip with one hand, pushing her down against him as he slowly completed his final thrust and held motionless. His stillness was followed almost instantly by a pulse she felt at her entrance, and she knew he was done.

She dropped her legs from his back and he eased down on top of her. She could still feel the pulsing expectation of her own desire, of her body seeking its own fulfillment. Russ's breath was warm and heavy against the side of her face, and within a minute it became heavier still.

Emma scowled. He'd fallen *asleep?*

She wiggled slightly. He murmured and lay one arm along her own, gripping her wrist for a moment and then subsiding.

Her unslaked desire roused a flame of annoyance. She'd been so close! This was the second time they'd had sex, and the second time she'd had to go to bed hungry for an orgasm.

She wiggled harder, and then shifted to slide more of his weight off her back.

He came groggily awake. "Oh, sorry." He pulled the pillow out from under her and then turned onto his back. She moved to get up, but he caught her arm. "No, come lie with me."

"I have to get the towel," she said, not wanting to give in to the sleepy comfort of a postcoital snuggle. It wasn't postanything for *her*.

His lips tightened, and the sleepiness began to clear from his eyes. "I should go clean up."

Her annoyance warred with her liking of him, and liking won out. She pushed against his chest, making him lie back again. "Don't be silly. I'll be just a moment. Stay here."

She cleaned herself up and removed her veil, then warmed a washcloth in hot water and carried it back to him, cleaning him of the vestiges of their lovemaking. She set the cloth aside and climbed up onto the bed with him, letting him settle her against his side. She pulled lengths of silk up over them and then rested her palm and cheek against his chest.

He reached over and stroked his hand down her side. "You need to have your turn."

She closed her eyes and shook her head. "That's not what this is about."

His hand moved over her hip and down to the edge of her sex. "I'll enjoy it more if I know that you enjoy it."

It was what she'd wanted five minutes ago, not now. Her mood was gone and some perverse part of her wanted to wallow in the injustice of the orgasm score. "I do enjoy it. Very much," she said, with a hair less conviction than might have been believable.

"Don't do that."

She tucked her face against him, knowing what he meant but asking anyway. "Don't do what?"

"Say things you plainly don't mean. Be honest with me, Emma. You've nothing to lose by telling me the truth."

She opened her eyes, staring at the hairs on his chest, and gathered the courage for honesty. "I do enjoy it. But I was very close to enjoying it a lot more—if you know what I mean."

He squeezed her arm. "Tell me when it's like that, so I can do something about it. Will you tell me?"

She nodded, but it was so much easier to try to please someone else, rather than ask another to please you.

"Promise?" he asked.

"Promise."

It was a promise she didn't know if she could keep.

Nine

Russ's world narrowed to the scraping of his skates on the ice and the rasp of his breathing inside his helmet. Skate full-bore to the blue line, stop on the outside edge of his skate, cross his other leg over, skate back to the goal line, stop on outside edge of skate, cross over, skate to red line, stop, cross over, skate, stop. He was doing line drills while his fellow players showered and dressed after the final game.

Skate, stop, cross over, skate. Stopping on the outside edge of his skate strained the inner muscles of his thighs and the crossover demanded concentration and agility. The sprints from line to line sucked every last dreg of energy from his muscles. It was all he could think to do, to force thoughts of Emma from his mind. Thoughts of her, thoughts of the things they'd done together, thoughts of how he had forgotten who he was as he chased her through the apartment, his only goal to capture her nearly nude body, toss it down, and plunge himself inside it until the steel-hard ache in his loins was eased.

He'd turned into an animal!

Skate, stop, cross over, skate. It had been a favorite drill of his coach when he'd first learned to play, and had also been his coach's favorite punishment when he thought his team needed to get their act together.

He needed to get *his* act together. That sexually aggressive side of himself had frightened him afterward, realizing how slim his control was over his baser nature; how thin the wall was between civilized behavior and barbaric.

Worse yet was knowing that last night's escapade was just a mild version of what he would be capable of, given the proper circumstance. If he'd been born a thousand years ago and given a sword and a village to plunder . . .

Skate, stop, cross over, skate. And what about Emma? Had she gotten off on that power play? Well, technically she hadn't, though she'd complained that she'd gotten close.

He didn't know if he could handle many more nights like that. The role-playing, the freaky ideas, never knowing what to expect, never certain if he'd be able to perform—and aware that he'd left her unsatisfied twice now.

He coasted to a stop, winded, feeling the nausea of overexertion. Crap. He used to be able to go twice as long. He was getting old.

The pop of a beer can being opened echoed across the ice, and he turned and saw Greg standing in the box with a beer in his hand, another sitting on top of the boards.

"Want a beer?" Greg called across the ice.

Russ skated over to him and climbed over the boards, propping his stick in a corner. He pulled off his gloves and helmet and took the can, popping the top and taking a gulp.

"Whatcha doing? Training for the senior Olympics?" Greg asked, taking a seat on the bench.

Russ joined him, wiping sweat off his brow with the back of his wrist. "I've been eating too well lately. Got to fight off the belly." The Zamboni driver started up the machine and moved it onto the ice.

"Business dinners?"

Russ shook his head, watching the Zamboni begin its pattern of ice-cleaning and repair. "No."

"A shopping trip to Costco? Those giant muffins, man, they'll kill you."

Russ chuckled. "No, I've gone out a couple times."

"You mean *out* out? Like with a member of the opposite sex?"

Russ nodded.

Greg slapped him on the back. "Finally! Russell has a girlfriend! Congratulations!" He lifted his beer can and clunked it against Russ's.

"Don't register me for wedding gifts yet. I doubt things will last the week."

"Hey, stop with the half-empty view. You've got a living

female willing to go out with you more than once! You should be offering prayers of thanks."

They were silent for a moment while the Zamboni roared by in front of them.

"So who is she? That younger woman you talked about? The one who was cleaning your house?"

Russ nodded.

"And she actually likes you?"

He shrugged. "I don't know."

"Are you going to see her again?"

"Tomorrow night."

"What date number is it?"

"Three."

"You're golden, man! If she hasn't done it already, she's probably planning to jump you."

Russ laughed. "Maybe."

"Women usually wait till the third date. They don't want you to think they're cheap."

"Where did you pick up this bit of wisdom?"

"*Men's Health* magazine. But everyone knows about the third-date thing."

"I can't believe you read that crap. It's *Cosmo* for guys."

"Hey, I'm a well-informed, balanced male," Greg said, buffing his nails on his chest. "A veritable Renaissance man."

Russ choked and Greg pounded his back, making him slosh beer onto the back of his hand.

"Sorry, man. Hey, if you make it past date three and she's

still talking to you after she sees that tiny mushroom you call a dick, maybe the wife and I can have you two over to dinner. Tina would love that. She's always asking why you aren't seeing anyone."

"I don't think this is going to be that type of relationship. She's made it clear that she's not looking for anything permanent."

Greg stared at him. "You are *so* lucky. So fucking lucky, I can't believe it. Where's the justice?"

"The justice is that you can grow a beer gut and Tina won't leave you."

"That's right," Greg said, patting his gut. "I'm losing my hair, too. And she's noticed the hair growing out of my dad's ears and nose, and swears she's going to trim mine when it gets that way. Yep, she's good and stuck with me."

"It will be a long time before Emma is stuck with anyone, and that's the way she wants it."

Greg belched. "Her loss."

Russ arched a brow and refrained from comment. He didn't know what was going on in Emma's head, but he was sure that the last thing on her "I Want" list was trimming a man's nose hairs for the next sixty years.

Emma sidestepped a transient sitting on the sidewalk and continued along Second Avenue. Belltown was host to a fair share of homeless folk and day laborers waiting to be picked up in drive-by hirings. None of them had ever paid the least attention to her, though, so she was beginning to get used to their presence and no longer steeled her nerves to walk by them.

It was Wednesday afternoon, and she had nothing to do but think about her design for the train station. She'd spent all yesterday preparing for tonight with Russ, including buying the latex gloves she'd need for one rather surprising sexual technique she'd read about, and she knew her preparations were an excuse to avoid her drafting table, computer, and sheets of paper covered with lousy concepts.

This morning she'd cleaned the bathroom and washed every bit of laundry she could think of. She'd vacuumed and polished her grandmother's silver. She'd watched the noon news and tried to engross herself in an episode of *Emeril* on the Food Network. Eventually, though, she'd forced herself to sit down in front of her sketch pad.

And there she'd sat, staring, until twenty minutes had passed and she'd pushed away in disgust. A walk seemed like a good idea, and maybe taking another look at King Street Station would inspire her.

She'd been walking about twenty minutes when her cell phone rang. "Hello?"

"Emma?"

"Yes?"

"Hi! This is Kevin. Remember, Kevin from Russ's house?"

"Oh, hi. Yes, I remember."

"I was just calling to see how you've been, and if you got moved in all right."

"Yes, everything's fine. The new place is great."

"Good! Where is it, anyway?"

"Downtown."

"What part?"

"Belltown."

"Nice area. Russ used to have a place there."

"Mmm."

"I hear traffic. Are you on the road?"

"No, I'm walking. I'm at Pioneer Square."

"Really? I'm about six blocks from there! Have you had lunch?"

"A snack," Emma mumbled, unable to lie.

"Do you have some free time? I know a great little Vietnamese place in the International District."

"Actually, I wanted to finish my walk. I want to go look at the train station."

"The station? Why?"

She explained about the design contest.

"How about I meet you there, then? It's just a few blocks from the station to the restaurant. We could go there when you're done looking around."

"Kevin, I think you need to know that I'm seeing someone."

He was silent for a long moment. "Someone serious?"

"Not really. We've been going out for only a week. But I'm not the type of person who can date more than one guy at a time."

"Ah. Okay." Another long moment of silence passed.

"Well, would you still consider having lunch with me, just as a friend?"

"You don't have to do that."

"I'd like to. It's good to have friends of the opposite sex, don't you think?"

Emma felt her stomach rumble. "I've only had Vietnamese food once, but I did like it."

"Great! I'll meet you at the station in about twenty minutes? Will that give you enough time?"

"Sure. That'd be great." Emma said good-bye and closed the phone, regretting already that she'd agreed to lunch. He seemed like a nice enough guy, but she was going to have to be careful not to let something slip about Russ. She'd have to keep the conversation focused on Kevin, and hope he was like most guys and loved to talk about himself.

She picked up her pace to cover the last couple of blocks to the station quickly. She didn't want Kevin with her, distracting her, as she looked around and tried to call down divine inspiration from the gods of Amtrak and the Burlington Northern Santa Fe railroad.

When she got there, she stood for a while across the street, mentally matching the maps and site diagrams from the contest website to what she was seeing before her. The station had been built in 1906 by the same architects who'd done Grand Central Station in New York City.

Now it was just a mess. Except for the clock tower, you couldn't tell that the place was a station, and couldn't see how to get to it by car or even how to enter it by foot, since the entrance across the elevated street was barricaded with chain-link gates. You wouldn't guess that you had to find a stairwell beside a building half a block away to get to the station one story lower, or drive a block and a half west and circle around a block of unrelated buildings.

So. Necessity number one: improve access.

Two: make it obvious that this is the station.

Three:

Three. Hmm.

The place needed to be clean and attractive; welcoming, comfortable, and convenient. Efficient to move through. Interesting to wait in, and calming to soothe the nerves of irritated travelers.

What aesthetic would achieve that? She didn't know if she should try to revive the old Edwardian Era station—the historic photos she'd seen on the web were beautiful—or go for something purely modern Northwest. She didn't know what the people of Seattle would prefer. She didn't know what *she* would prefer, and didn't know what else she should be thinking about but wasn't.

Well, she'd watched *The Apprentice* and had learned the value of market research.

Twenty minutes later, she'd talked to three passengers sitting in the waiting area and to two Amtrak employees. The brief conversations had been revealing. They wanted natural light instead of the boarded-up windows. They wanted a

shop with magazines and snacks. They wanted time sched-
ules posted where you could see them. And those who lived
in Seattle wanted their station to impress visitors and give
them a taste of the region.

She was standing in the middle of the crowded, dirty
waiting area, staring up at the stained acoustical tiles and
fluorescent lights overhead, when Kevin found her.

"Emma! Hi! I hope I didn't keep you waiting!" He trotted
up to her with an eager puppy dog look.

"Hi, Kevin."

"Are you done here?"

"I think so." She would have liked to stay longer, but she
wouldn't be able to think with him trailing her.

"I don't want to rush you."

"No, it's okay. I've seen what I needed to."

As they climbed the stairs up to the street, he asked, "So,
how's the house-cleaning business going?"

"It's going all right. I've cut back so that I can work on
this train station project."

"Yeah? Still cleaning Russ's place, though?"

"No. He didn't really need a housekeeper." She slanted a
glance at him, curious how he would take that news.

"Did he fire you?"

"Not really. We mutually decided that he could clean his
own house."

"Yeah, he's a neat freak. A perfectionist. I didn't know
why his sister hired you in the first place. She should have

known that the last thing Russ would want was someone coming in and messing with his stuff."

"A perfectionist? Really? I didn't get that impression." She was intrigued.

"Maybe you weren't around him long enough. He's the type of guy who can't stand loose threads, vagueness. He wants things done right, planned out. He's big on process. He wants everything to follow a process."

"No freewheeling creativity?"

"Not if it means things aren't being ticked off the checklist on schedule. I think he believes that even art can be created according to a timeline."

"So from your tone, I take it that you work differently?"

He grinned. "I'm more laid-back."

And that was the reason Russ owned a company that he'd started himself, and Kevin was only an employee. And would always be an employee.

"Oh, we're here! This is the restaurant." Kevin opened the glass door at the end of a dismal little strip mall.

The smells as they entered did much to allay Emma's misgivings. The decor wasn't much, but the place was busy, most of the older customers Asian and speaking what she assumed to be Vietnamese. A young Asian woman greeted them in English and showed them to a table.

Emma glanced over the menu, recognized nothing, and set it aside. "You're familiar with the food, so you can order for me. I'll eat anything except green bell peppers."

They chatted for a minute about what to get, and then the waitress came and took their order, appearing again a minute later with iced tea for both of them.

"So is Russ hard to work for?" Emma asked as she dumped Splenda into her glass and stirred it with her straw. "Just what do you do at his company anyway?"

"I'm a senior account manager. And Russ is great, as long as you do your job the way he thinks it should be done."

"A micromanager?" If so, he must leave the tendency at the office. He had let her do whatever she wished these past nights and seemed to trust her to make decisions on her own.

"If he thinks things have gone off track, yeah, he spells out exactly what he thinks you should be doing."

Emma murmured a noncommittal sound, wondering if Russ got on Kevin's case because Kevin needed a whip cracked over his head to keep from being a total screwup.

"I'll feel sorry for whoever marries him," Kevin went on, grinning. "He'd tell her exactly how he wanted the house kept, how the kids should be raised, which groceries to buy; probably even examine her checkbook to be sure it was balanced."

Emma raised an eyebrow, wondering if Kevin was serious about his ideas of what wives were for. It apparently hadn't occurred to him that Russ might marry a woman who worked outside the home. It also wasn't helping her opinion of Kevin that he was all but badmouthing his boss and friend.

"But you like him, overall?" she asked.

Kevin shrugged. "You can't not like him. I mean, the guy's a straight shooter and as determined as a Sherman tank. And he's not going to let his personal feelings get in the way of doing what he thinks is right. And he's loyal."

"He sounds like a fine, upstanding citizen. Not very exciting, though," she said, baiting him to say more. "Not much of a risk taker."

"No, James was the one who was daring, who was willing to take a gamble. That was his brother—do you know about that?"

"Yes."

"James was the visionary, but his ideas probably wouldn't have come to much without Russ there to do the grunt work. And when their first business, usedbooks.com, started to go under, it was Russ who saw that some of their proprietary software was worth salvaging. Enough about him, though. Tell me more about this design contest."

Emma did, keeping it as brief and impersonal as possible. She didn't want to tell Kevin about her creative struggles. He didn't give her the same sense of being an emotionally safe sounding board that Russ did.

Their salad rolls arrived while she was talking, and by the time those were finished and their enormous bowls of *pho*—noodle soup—had arrived she was trying to turn the conversation back to him. "So, how's your car treating you?"

"All right. But I'm beginning to think it was a mistake. It

looks too middle-aged. I'd be better off with something like that beefed-up Honda of yours."

"I'll trade ya."

He laughed. "What type of car do you think I should get?"

"For attracting women?"

He nodded.

"It doesn't really work that way. Not if you're looking for a serious relationship. Are you?"

"I'd like to get married." He looked at her soulfully.

"Well if that's what you want, forget about impressing women with your car. Buy one that you honestly love and are excited about. If you didn't give a rat's ass about what anyone thought of you, what would you buy? What's the first thing that comes to mind?"

"Hmm . . ."

"No, tell me. Now! Don't think about it."

"A Mini."

Emma blinked. "One of those new Mini Coopers?" It was a chick car, even cuter than the new VW Bugs.

He nodded, looking hopeful.

"Then that's what you should get. The right woman will appreciate your choice and be impressed that you had the courage to choose what suited you, rather than the biggest, fastest penis car you could afford."

His face colored. "Penis car?"

She slurped up a mouthful of noodles. "You think

women can't see through a guy's car choices?" she said when she'd swallowed. "We assume that penis cars are driven by insecure, arrogant assholes. With a *Mini*, though, a woman would think, 'There's a man who'd make a kind, attentive, and good-humored dad.' "

"Yeah?"

"Yeah."

"So what does your new boyfriend drive?"

She blinked. "Er, some sort of hybrid, I think. I haven't been in it yet, though."

"Russ has one of those."

"Mmm?" she murmured, quickly stuffing her mouth with noodles.

"He donates to a lot of environmental causes. Sierra Club, all that. So is that the type of guy you like, one who drives a hybrid?"

She shrugged, stuffing more noodles into her mouth. He waited for her to swallow. She took her time. "All I want to know," she said at last, "is that it's paid for and it runs."

"So what does your car say about you?"

She laughed. "That I take what I can get." She explained about her brother and his cautious wife.

"What would *you* buy if money were no object and you didn't care what anyone would think?"

"I don't know."

"Yes, you do. Tell me," he insisted, echoing her earlier command to him.

A classic convertible roadster from the 1920s zipped through her imagination, roaring along a country road in England. It zipped and was gone, the impracticality of it erasing it from her mind. "A Volvo station wagon."

His eyes widened. "Really?"

"They're safe and you can haul a lot of stuff."

He didn't say anything.

Emma took a moment to think about her choice, then covered her face with her hands. "Oh God. That's pathetic."

"No, it's, er . . . practical. A very reasonable car. It sounds as if you're looking forward to being a wife and mother."

Emma groaned and pulled her hands down her face, stretching it into Edvard Munch's *The Scream*. "No! There will be time for that in my thirties. Why did I say a Volvo station wagon? Why? Why?"

"Maybe it's a secret longing."

She rolled her eyes. "Oh for God's sake. Not every woman is looking for a husband!"

"But if you find him before you think you're ready, maybe that means that you're more ready than you thought."

Emma dropped her hands. "What the hell are you talking about?"

"Maybe you've already found your Mr. Right." He stared at her with an infuriating expression of kindly patience, as if awaiting her inevitable acceptance of him as savior.

Emma pulled out her cell phone and checked the time.

"Jeez, it's getting late. I've got to get home. My *boyfriend* is coming over soon. Lunch has been great, though."

"You don't want dessert?" he asked, sitting up straight, the expression of calm wiped off his face.

"I'm stuffed—couldn't eat another bite. Thanks, though, I'll have to remember this place. Good food!" She dug in her purse, pulling out some cash.

"No, no, I invited you."

"That's kind of you." She looked him in the eye. "Thank you. Can I leave the tip?"

He shook his head and signaled for the check.

She accepted his offer of a ride back to her neighborhood and had him drop her a block and a half away from her building. He'd chattered about his favorite TV shows throughout the short drive, leaving her blissfully free to lose herself in her own thoughts. As she said good-bye and watched him drive off, the same thought plagued her that had plagued her throughout the drive.

A Volvo? What the hell was the matter with her?

Talk about thinking inside the box.

Cripes.

Ten

"Are you ready for your bed bath, Mr. Carrick?"

"Yes, nurse," Russ said, wondering why he hadn't put a stop to these skits, yet grateful that he hadn't. Emma was all in white: a white short-short zip-front dress, garter belt, stockings that came halfway up her thighs, spike heels, and a tiny white paper cap on her head with a red cross in the center.

He hoped she left the stocking-and-heels ensemble on through it all. Whether planted in the male psyche by adolescent perusals of *Playboy* or not, a woman in garter belt and spike heels did something electric to a man's lust. His gaze flicked between the cleavage of the tight dress and the hemline that barely covered her sex and butt cheeks.

Oh God. He was going to enjoy this too much.

"Roll onto your stomach, Mr. Carrick, if you would."

He did as bid under the sheet of her bed, and turned his

head so that he could watch her set a bowl of steaming water and a sea sponge down on her nightstand. There was also massage oil there, a plastic water carafe and cup, bottles of pills that looked like candy, a thermometer, a cheap pink stethoscope, and a pair of latex gloves. Props to add to the hospital effect, apparently, just like she'd found a hospital gown for him to wear. No man felt virile in a hospital gown, but he was willing to play the part in exchange for seeing her in that nurse's getup, and he had high hopes for the massage oil.

She pulled down the sheet and leaned over to untie the fastenings of his hospital gown. He reached out and stroked his fingertips along her thigh, tracing the place where stocking changed to flesh.

"*Tch tch*, Mr. Carrick. You know better than to flirt with your nurse."

He slid his hand up to the hem of her dress, reaching under it to lightly brush against the tropical warmth of her sex. She wasn't wearing underpants.

"*Very* naughty, Mr. Carrick," she said softly, pressing herself against his hand, allowing him to caress her. He heard her suck in a breath of pleasure, and a moment later she moved away, out of reach.

He closed his eyes, feeling absurdly happy. Good food, good wine, and a beautiful woman about to give him a bath and sex. Greg was right. He *was* a lucky bastard.

He heard her wring out the sponge, the droplets of water

the only sound in the apartment beyond their own breathing. The quiet created a strangely intimate intensity, each of Emma's sounds and movements capturing his attention. He could hear the brush of her arm against the fabric of her dress, the faint rub of one stocking-clad thigh against the other.

She started on his shoulders, rubbing gently with the steaming sponge. The water was hot enough to shock his skin, soon replaced with a chill as his damp skin was exposed to the air. The contrasts were weirdly pleasing, and the more so because he didn't know where to expect the sponge to hit next. Emma worked in a semirandom pattern but gradually made her way down his back, over his rump, and to his feet.

"Please turn over," she said softly.

He did so, freeing the erection that had been pressing with almost painful fullness against the mattress. He saw her eyes widen, and he bobbed it in greeting.

"Mr. Carrick, I don't know what you've been thinking, but I'm only here to wash you and massage any sore muscles."

A smile pulled at his mouth, but he refused to take the verbal bait.

"You don't have any areas that need special attention, do you?" she asked. "Any place at all?"

"I'll let you find it on your own."

She wrung out the sponge again and went to work on his

thigh, bringing it tauntingly close to his groin. "This is modern medicine, Mr. Carrick. Patients are supposed to work *with* their health care professionals in order to receive the best treatment possible."

"I think you're doing pretty well on your own."

She climbed onto the bed, straddling his legs as she worked the sponge up his belly. "You think so?"

He pulled the pillow under his head so he had a better view. Her breasts were nearly spilling out of the neckline, and the hem of her dress had ridden up her hips, revealing her sex, the glorious warmth of it hovering mere inches above his body. She moved up his body several inches, her mound brushing against his erection.

He slid his hands up the outsides of her thighs, then around back to cup her buttocks. She leaned forward, her hands on his chest.

"You really shouldn't be doing that, Mr. Carrick."

He reached farther and found the silky warmth of her folds, skimming his fingertips along them. He watched her face, her eyes closing, her lips parting.

"Open your dress," he said softly.

She met his gaze, her eyes dark with arousal, then lifted one hand off his chest to tug down her zipper.

"There," he said when the zipper was at midtorso. He reached up and slid it off her shoulders, trapping her arms at her sides, her breasts coming free. He lowered his hands to her hips and urged her farther up his body.

A frown pinched her brows. "What are you doing, Mr. Carrick?"

"Assisting." He continued to walk her upward on her knees until she was forced to step over his shoulders, at which point the light dawned.

"Oh, no, Russ. No, you can't mean to—"

"Shh. The other patients will hear you."

She grabbed the headboard for balance, her arms still partway pinned by her dress. She looked down at him, her face framed by the mounds of her breasts, and started again to protest. He gripped her hips and laid his tongue to her folds. He wouldn't let her get through this night without an orgasm.

Emma's words shimmered into nothingness as the sensation of Russ's tongue on her sex rushed through her. Still, she felt self-conscious as she straddled his face and hung onto the headboard, her thighs straining to keep in position above him. He could see so *much* of her from down there; his view upward must be of her tummy. She felt exposed and alone, but when she looked down, she found him watching her, only his eyes and forehead visible. She was embarrassed that he was watching her while he licked her.

She felt his tongue find the right spot and swirl, and she had to look away from the intensity of his eyes. She turned her head to the side and closed her eyes, trying to forget that he was there.

His tongue became something else in her mind: a nameless tool used to give her pleasure as she straddled it; as she was forced to accept its touch whether she wanted to or not. It was easy to imagine herself elsewhere this way, with her eyes closed and no contact with him beyond that warm mouth on her sex and the firm grip of his hands on her hips.

His wet, warm tongue stroked up and down her folds, parting them, then skimming their edges. He flattened his tongue and laved the length of her, almost too hard, trapping her between pleasure and discomfort. The tip of his tongue played at her opening, rubbing gently until she parted to admit a bare breath of tongue. He moved up again and sucked at her nub, his tongue teasing it with gentle flicks inside the tight, sucking confines of his lips. She gripped the rail of the headboard and tightened the muscles of her thighs, straining toward the pleasure. The flicking of his tongue was light enough to make her press her hips toward him, asking for more even as she knew that harder would not feel as good as this taunting, teasing touch.

She was suddenly impatient for him to thrust himself deep within her, touching places that no tongue could reach, with that thick, stretching width that satisfied the way no fingers could.

She wrenched herself away from his mouth, dismounting. "There's something I want to do to you," she said before he could protest, reaching over him for the massage oil and the gloves.

"If you wish. I was quite happy where I was, though."

She gave him a small smile, not sure of the truth of that, and pulled on the gloves. As much as she wanted him to give her an orgasm, part of her also *didn't* want it. There was power in being the one to give and not receive. She was in control: of him, of herself, of how much of her inner self she revealed. She could find plenty of pleasure without reaching that big O.

"You'll be even happier when I'm through with you," she said, raising an eyebrow suggestively as she unzipped her dress the rest of the way and shrugged it off.

Naked on top, with only the garter belt, stockings, and spike heels below, she poured massage oil into her gloved palm and warmed it between her hands. She cupped her breasts in her slick hands and coated them in oil, watching as his gaze followed every move. The oil smelled of lavender; it was supposed to be a turn-on for men.

She put her hands on him and started kneading his chest and shoulders, then worked her way down his arms to his hands, taking her time, running her fingers between his and massaging the webs, the joints, the center of his palm. He made small happy sounds of pleasure.

She went to his feet next and gave them the same treatment, running her thumb hard along his arch, pulling gently on his toes, and giving a soft pinching massage to the two indentations on either side of his Achilles tendon. Up his calf, over his knee, and then to his thighs, working gradually up them until she reached his balls. She cupped them in her hands and stroked them with infinite care, then lay down beside him on her side, her mouth level with his groin.

She glanced up at him, meeting his eyes as she reached over his hip and urged him to turn onto his side, facing her. He obeyed, and she wrapped her lower hand around the base of his erection and put his head to her lips. She pressed her tongue against the underside of his cock, making her tongue as firm as a thumb as she moved her mouth up and down on him.

She felt his reaction in his body, in the tensing of his muscles and the movement of his hips as he thrust into her mouth. She slowed and sped up, took him shallow and took him deep, her jaw beginning to ache. She settled into a deep steady rhythm as her upper hand slid over his hip, over his buttock, and toward that dark passage where she had never ventured before with anyone.

The book she'd bought *said* this was a good idea. It said that the prostate was a man's secret G-spot, and that stroking it with a finger up his ass would propel him to sky-rocketing explosions that he'd never known before.

His breathing was growing ragged, and she knew that if she was going to send him shooting for the moon, now was the time. Her gloved finger, slick with massage oil, found his tight entrance and dove deep inside.

His reaction was immediate and spectacular.

"*Yeeow!*" he cried, and reached back to knock her hand away. "*What the hell? What was that?*" He wasn't thrusting into her mouth anymore. His whole body felt like a piece of lumber, board hard and not moving anywhere.

Her hand curled into a fist as if to hide its shame and she tucked her face against his thigh in embarrassment. "You didn't like it," she said into his leg.

"What?" he asked. "I can't hear you." She felt his hands on her shoulder and head, guiding her to look up at him.

She rolled away and sat up. "You didn't like that?" she asked.

"No!" He rolled onto his back, staring at the ceiling.

She bit her lip. "Not at all?"

"No!"

"The book said it would feel good."

"I don't care what the book said!" he said, looking at her. "I don't want you putting your—putting your—I don't want you touching me there!"

She looked down at her gloved hands, feeling like a pervert. Worse, she felt like she'd failed. "It's supposed to feel really, really good," she said, trying to salvage her efforts.

"Emma, I don't care. I'm never going to enjoy anything that involves putting something up my—well, up there. I just can't."

She raised her eyes to his. "Have you ever tried?"

"No!"

"No girlfriend has ever done this to you?"

"No! And I'm never going to let one!"

"Why not?"

"Because!"

She raised her brows. Was he embarrassed? "Because—"

"Because I don't want you anywhere near that spot."

"Because?"

"Because it's not a nice place."

"In what way, not nice?" she asked. "Not nice because it's naughty?"

"I don't care about that. I care about . . ."

"Yes?"

"It's dirty. Unhygienic."

She held up her hand. "But I'm wearing a glove."

He groaned and covered his face with his arms. Strangely, his erection was still present.

"You don't need to worry about it being dirty if I have a glove, and if I don't mind doing it."

He groaned again.

"Don't you want to let me try? Aren't you a little bit curious?"

He lowered his arms and looked at her. "Emma. No."

"*I'm* curious. I'd like to know if you'd enjoy it."

"You're wearing a nurse's cap. Hints of the medical profession, a latex glove, plus a finger *there* is about as far from sexual excitement as a guy can get. If I wanted my prostate examined I'd pay my primary care doctor to do it, and he wouldn't expect me to enjoy it."

"A lot of men supposedly do—not the exam, but the finger thing during sex."

"Emma, it's not an area of my anatomy that I wish to explore in a sexual way. The reasons why don't matter. That part of my body is off limits, permanently."

She shrugged and peeled off the gloves, careful to turn them inside out as she did so. She was a little hurt that he wasn't willing to give it a try. It seemed that she was the one who had been taking the bigger risk, and it would have been nice if he'd met her halfway. "Okay. I thought you wanted new things, is all. You said you wanted me to be creative."

"Come here," he said, opening his arms.

She crawled back into place beside him, lying on her side against his torso, her arm over his chest. "I only wanted to please you," she said, playing with his nipple, tugging lightly at the hairs around it. She found it a little easier to talk if she didn't look at his face. "If this didn't please you, then tell me what would."

Russ put his arm around Emma's shoulders; she was obviously upset. There was nothing more embarrassing for him than a detailed analysis of his sexual behaviors and preferences, yet that was what she was asking for.

"You don't need to be quite so, er, theater-oriented about the sex," he managed. "I don't need costumes and a script, or choreographed dance sequences." He felt her flinch, and grimaced at his social clumsiness. But how else was he supposed to say it? "The costumes have been fun," he said, trying to soften the criticism. "You've looked wonderful in them, and I especially like the, er, garter belt bit."

"Yeah?"

"Yes. It's very nice. But beyond a bit of sexy lingerie, my tastes are pretty tame. Vanilla. White bread. Even bland."

"What about all that creativity you asked for?"

The creativity that he'd meant to describe his *dinner*, not sex. "I guess I was wrong about what I'd like."

"So, what do you want? Do you want the missionary position each time?"

What I want is to have sex with you—*Emma Mayson. Not a harem girl or Betty Crocker with a bowl of pudding.* But it wasn't part of their arrangement that he ask for access to her inner self. It was her body he had hired, and her body she had agreed to let him see naked and to touch, not the person inside.

"I'm open to other positions. Let's just stay away from the accessories and the scripts and, er, the advanced sexual techniques. We don't have to work our way through *The Joy of Sex.*"

He felt her sigh, her breath warm on his skin. "I didn't really want to put my finger in there," she said softly.

Relief went through him. He'd been afraid she must think him a conservative old prude. "Then why'd you do it?"

"Because I let the book tell me what to do."

"Emma, I'm not going to enjoy something if you don't.

Trust your instincts next time. We should only do what pleases us both."

She was quiet. A minute or more passed.

"Emma? Are you awake?"

She laughed softly. "Yes. Just thinking."

"About?"

She shook her head against him. "Just thinking."

He rolled over on top of her, bracing his weight on his elbows and knees, and looked down into her eyes. "Too much thinking has gotten us into this mess. Let's abandon it for a while."

A smile pulled at the corners of her mouth. "How about you show me what *your* instincts are telling you? Maybe I'll learn something."

"Probably not, but it could be fun anyway."

Her grin widened, and she wrapped one leg around his waist. It was all the invitation he needed.

Eleven

H ow's the seduction of your landlord going?" Beth asked
from her incarceration on her living room sofa. Her
legs were propped onto pillows and her belly looked as big as
a cooler chest. She had preeclampsia and was on bed rest.

"Seduction? What seduction?" Daphne asked, coming in
from Beth's kitchen with a tray loaded with lemonade,
sliced fruit, and a bowl of cream cheese dip.

"Emma has been trying to seduce her landlord. Some hot
older guy with a pile of money," Beth said, her eyes following the tray of food.

"Emma! Why didn't you tell me?" Daphne asked, setting
the tray on the coffee table and pulling a seat up close.

"The seduction is successful," Emma said, putting together a small plate of fruit and dip and handing it to Beth.

"Bless you, my child," Beth said in fervent gratitude. "So
you slept with him?"

Daphne punched Emma on the shoulder. "No way! Emma, you devil!"

"Yes, I slept with him." Emma arched her brow, enjoying their reactions. "And we're still seeing each other."

"How many times have you done it?" Beth asked.

"I don't *count*!"

"That many!" Daphne said. "I *knew* you had a wild thing inside you, Emma."

"We've been seeing each other a few times a week for the past three weeks," she said, allowing herself to brag. It felt nice to finally be the one with boy gossip to share, instead of so often being the one who listened and provided the understanding ear.

"Oh my God," Beth said. "Is this turning into something serious, or are you still trying to keep him as just your fuck buddy?"

"Fuck buddy?" Daphne asked, stunned. "*You* have a fuck buddy?"

"Don't *call* it that! Say he's my . . . my lover."

"Why did you want this guy as a fu—*lover* instead of as a boyfriend?" Daphne asked. "Is he an asshole who just happens to be great in the sack?"

"No, he's quite nice, actually. And good-looking. But he's ten years older, and rich, and we live in different worlds. A boyfriend-girlfriend relationship wouldn't make any sense," Emma explained, though most of the time she didn't remember that there was an age difference between them, and they always found plenty of things to talk about, whether personal, political, or cultural. Their ways of looking at the world were surprisingly similar, and the knowledge that he was rich and owned a company had faded into the background.

Russ seemed thoroughly at ease in her—in *his*—apartment, and seemed to like being there better than being in his own beautiful home. Each time he came over, she could see in the space of five or ten minutes how he began to relax, his tension uncoiling from his shoulders, the focused expression on his face softening. He made himself at home in her kitchen and her living room to a degree she hadn't seen in his own house, and he was staying with her for longer and longer after they had sex. She could only think that he didn't want to go back to his big empty house.

"Ten years is nothing," Daphne said. "He's cute and rich and single—he *is* single, isn't he?—and a nice guy. Why the hell wouldn't you want more from him than sex?"

"I'm working on my career."

Daphne rolled her eyes. "There's enough time in the day for both work and romance, you know. Right, Beth?"

Beth blew a raspberry and gestured at her belly. "Yeah, right. Look where that got *me!*"

"I didn't say she had to get pregnant. Just that she could fit romance in."

"You haven't found that you've devoted less energy to work since you got involved with Derek?" Emma asked.

Daphne made a face. "Derek."

"Things aren't going well?" Beth asked.

Daphne shrugged one shoulder. "Maybe they're going how they always go when two people move in together. It's the first time I've lived with a guy, so I don't know what's normal and what's not."

"Talk to the expert," Beth said. "Come on, spill to Mama. What's he doing?"

"It's more what he's *not* doing. None of the cooking or grocery shopping. None of the laundry or housekeeping. I mean, the guy's house was clean and he fed himself before I moved in. What happened that suddenly he needs a maid?"

Beth snorted. "Sounds normal."

Emma thought of her own evenings with Russ. He helped out with the dirty dishes and some of the dinner preparation, but she wasn't sure he'd continue doing that if he had a wife. She could imagine him happily leaving it all to her, if she didn't protest.

"He's not being as affectionate, either," Daphne said. "He doesn't call me three times a day like he did before. He doesn't leave me little notes. He wants sex just as often—or more often—but it's not as good. It's like he's using me to get off, and doesn't care whether I have a good time."

"Normal," Beth said.

"Really?" Emma asked in dismay. "Is that really what it's like, for everyone?"

But weren't her nights with Russ already headed in that direction? They had settled into an easy pattern of dinner and conversation, lingering over dessert and coffee before they headed for her bedroom. Ever since the prostate incident she let him take the lead in sex, with the result that their joinings were now unremarkable in the techniques, but far less stressful in the planning and execution. She was relieved not to strive to make each night an unforgettable sexual extravaganza. A part of her missed the scripts and costumes, though: it was easier to pretend to be a wanton sexpot than it was to let him see her true, natural enjoyment of sex without the shelter of a disguise.

And she still hadn't had an orgasm. He seemed to have given up forcing one on her, which both suited her and, perversely, annoyed her. He was an attentive and considerate lover, giving her plenty of foreplay, yet for reasons she didn't fully understand, she refused to let him bring her to that ultimate point of release.

Maybe she was punishing herself. Maybe she was punishing *him*. Maybe she liked the power. Who knew?

"I'm never going to get married if all it means is a slow decline into drudgery and bad sex," she said.

Beth shrugged. "Marriage has its advantages."

"Like?"

"He takes care of the cars." Beth took a sip of lemonade.

"That's it?" Emma asked.

"I'm thinking! It's hard to think when you're pregnant. Let's see. He takes out the garbage."

"And?"

"He pays the bills, including the mortgage."

"And?" Emma insisted. She needed to hear that Beth and Ty had a strong relationship. She needed to know that a friend of hers was succeeding at marriage, and was happy despite her grousing, because if Beth succeeded, then someday she, too, could succeed at it and be happy.

"And *what*? Emma, I don't know what you want to hear. He helps around the house, but I feel like his mother, nagging him to do each and every little thing. I feel like I'm an ugly, bulbous, enormous whale of a burden on him that he wishes would fall down a well! And I'm *mean* to him." Tears started to trickle down Beth's cheeks, and she snuffled, wiping at her nose with the back of her hand. "I say the meanest things to him, but all I really want is for him to hold me and tell me he loves me and everything is going to be okay, the baby is going to be okay, we're going to be okay, that *life* is going to be okay! But he hides from me and then I yell some more and call him names, and it's awful!"

Beth sobbed into the silence that followed.

"Good job, Emma," Daphne said. "Making the pregnant woman cry."

"I'm sorry," Emma said quietly. She reached over and touched Beth's arm. "I'm sorry. I didn't mean to upset you."

Beth sniffed in a long soggy breath. "It's not your fault." She smiled, then laughed shakily. "What type of friend am I? Every time I see you guys, I end up bawling. What a downer. I'm surprised you come see me at all."

181

Emma snorted. "As if we could stay away! You're the first friend I've had who was pregnant. Sheer curiosity will keep me coming back, no matter how weepy you get."

"And when the baby is born?"

"I haven't had a friend who had a baby, either. You're stuck with me, girl."

"Me too," Daphne said. "No matter what else is going on, it's still exciting that you're having a baby."

"Thanks."

The conversation wandered for a bit; then Daphne asked Emma how the job search was going.

Emma hunched her shoulders. "No progress."

"What are you going to do?"

Emma sighed and explained about the train station contest. "I know it's a long shot, but it's the only thing I can think of."

"There might not be that many people or firms who enter," Daphne pointed out. "Maybe you just have to beat out a few of them, to make it to the final ten."

"I'm tempted to be insulted."

"*Phht!* You know I didn't mean it that way."

"I know. And actually, I hope you're right, because so far I have zilch in the way of a great design. The deadline is only two weeks away."

"You've got nothing?" Beth asked.

"I have pieces of a design, ideas, but no overall vision. No grand, breathtaking, groundbreaking scheme. Nothing that makes you go 'Wow! That's incredible! Who's the genius who designed this?' "

"Aren't you asking a lot of yourself?" Daphne asked.

Emma threw up her hands. "How else am I going to get anyone's attention? I have to do something spectacular!"

"You've always been such a perfectionist," Beth said. "I'll bet you discard three-quarters of your ideas before they ever get to paper because you don't think they're good enough."

"So I'm discriminating."

"No, you're terrified of doing something that's less than perfect."

"But an architect *has* to be that way. Buildings fall down if architects aren't perfectionists."

Beth shrugged. "And look, you have no station idea that you think is good enough."

"It's true," Daphne said, nodding. "You're so careful, you never do anything daring."

Emma raised her brows. She'd like to hear what they thought of her daring if they knew the truth about Russ! "I've got a sex buddy. That's daring!"

"Is it?" Beth said. "I mean really, when you think about it, it seems a lot safer to keep a guy confined to one role in your life, than it is to take a risk like Daphne did and move in together."

"Hey, yeah!" Daphne agreed. "Are you afraid he won't like you enough to date you like a real girlfriend?"

"No," Emma lied.

"Have you seen him *at all* outside of your apartment?"

Emma pressed her lips shut.

"No?"

Emma scowled. "It's not part of our arrangement. Besides, he's busy."

"Busy doing what?" Beth asked.

"Well, like tonight. I believe he plays in an amateur hockey league tonight."

"Reeeally . . ." Daphne said. "Where?"

"A place called the Aurora Ice Arena."

Daphne nodded. "I think I've been by it. It's a twenty-minute drive from here." She grinned.

Emma's eyes widened. "No, you can't mean—"

"It's a brilliant idea!" Beth said from the couch.

"It's not! What's brilliant about it?" Emma cried.

"It's brilliant because it will entertain me to hear what happens when the two of you show up there. I'm sick of magazines and believe me, there's nothing good on TV. I need to be amused."

"You're not Queen Victoria, and we're not going," Emma stated.

"Always so safe in your box," Daphne said softly. "Safe where nothing can hurt you, but nothing interesting will happen to you, either."

Her words cut to Emma's core. It was true. Nothing exciting ever *did* happen to her, and she knew it was because she didn't let it. Caution and common sense and flat practicality were the laws of her life, and the terror of making an error was the guiding principle behind it all.

What a relief it would be to mess up and not care; to shrug her shoulders, say "Whoops!" and move on.

The need to make no wrong step kept her from taking any steps at all.

Emma chewed her lip. She *did* want to see Russ skate; she wanted to catch a glimpse of him in his normal life, at ease among friends. "We can go—"

Daphne shrieked. "Yes! Shall I drive? Do you want to drive?"

"We can go," Emma repeated, trying to scowl, but a smile tugging at her lips, "but we're not going to let him know we're there."

"What fun is that?" Daphne asked.

"Yeah, that's no good," Beth said.

"Hey, it's enough that I agreed to go! And it'll be fun; think of it as playing spy."

Daphne grumbled. "Fine. We'll be sneaky. He'll never know we were there."

"He better not. I don't want him to think I'm a psycho stalker."

"Don't worry," Daphne said, but there was something in her grin that Emma didn't trust.

She glanced at Beth. She wore the exact same grin.

Oh God.

Twelve

Russ lay on the bench in the locker room, dressed only in his black Puck Skins, and pulled his knee up to his chest, stretching. He'd arrived at the arena half an hour earlier than he usually did, hoping to ease the coiled tension of the day out of his muscles. Hoping as well to clear out distracting thoughts of Kevin and Emma.

He changed position, wishing he could stretch on the floor like you could in the Canadian ice rink locker rooms, where they washed the floors between each game. No one in their right mind would lie down on the locker room floor of the Aurora Ice Arena: it looked as if it hadn't been washed since the Cretaceous period, and the freestanding, stall-less toilet inexplicably plumbed into the center of the room was a reminder of just how filthy a hockey locker-room floor could get.

Still, this was home. The locker room might be a sty, the

ice might be soft and rutted, but this was where his surrogate family lived and he had a perverse affection for it. It was his haven. His sanctuary from the world. The place where he was not Russ Carrick, multimillionaire entrepreneur, but was simply Buffy.

One of his teammates came in and bobbed his chin in greeting. Russ grunted a reply and stood for a different stretch.

Unbidden, memories of his conversation with Kevin earlier in the day came back to mind.

"I think she's starting to like me," Kevin had said.

Russ had feigned disinterest, but his heart had thunked sickly in his chest. "How so?"

"Just a feeling I get, when I call her."

"Didn't you say she was seeing someone?"

Kevin's face had been impassive but strangely alert, as if watching for Russ's reaction. "She doesn't talk about him. It must not mean much to her if she doesn't talk about him."

Russ had shrugged, but the words had festered all day. Reason said that she was too cautious to talk about him to Kevin, even under cover of her mythical "boyfriend," but it gnawed at him that there was nothing she said to Kevin, not even a generic comment on their getting along well or liking some of the same things. It made him wonder whether she talked about him to her friends or pretended that he didn't exist.

Was he just a thrice weekly sex partner who ate the food

she prepared? The answer mattered more to him than he would have thought, and might help explain his faint, growing dissatisfaction when they had sex.

Emma still hadn't had an orgasm. Besides its being a constant insult to his sexual prowess, he was beginning to feel that she was holding back, that she was keeping the "real" Emma locked deep inside her while they were in bed. He sometimes got the uncomfortable sense that part of her was disengaged, watching from a distance and making dispassionate notes.

He shook his head, frustrated by his own desires. When his sister had hired Emma, he hadn't wanted her to clean his house. Later he hadn't wanted her to cook for him. Then he hadn't wanted her to be his mistress. Yet now look where he was: he wanted her to care about him when they were in bed together. He wanted her to love him, if just a little. Just enough that she would trust him and let him not just inside her body but inside her soul.

It wasn't what she wanted, though. She still swore that she had neither time nor energy for a romantic relationship and intended to devote herself to her career for several years.

She sounded like him in his twenties. Knowing how emotionally unreachable he had been to his girlfriends at that time, it felt like cosmic revenge.

At least he knew what his options were. He could keep her locked away in one small part of his life, his feelings for her under tight control, never allowed to grow beyond friendly affection. Or he could break off the affair and move on, finding someone who was ready for more.

He knew which was the wise choice and also that he wasn't prepared to make it. Like his long-suffering girl-friends of the past, he suspected it would take a certain length and depth of misery before self-preservation would kick in. That, or something would have to go drastically wrong between them. A fight, a lie, a betrayal. Something to make the relationship less attractive and give him a chance to break free, or make her decide to end it herself.

The locker room was filling up now, voices raised in cheerful rowdiness. Chuck—short for "upchuck"—hurried past to one of the toilets that had a stall, to rid himself of pregame jitters. Greg waved a greeting as he quick-stepped by, his nerves affecting him in an even less pleasant way.

And yet they loved the game and called this home. He shook his head. Love never made any sense.

"Do you see him?" Daphne asked.

Emma sank lower in the hard plastic seat and carefully looked over her shoulder at the ice where masked hockey players in mismatched, unlabeled jerseys were milling around the ice, slapping pucks and warming up. "No, I can't tell which one he is. I'm not even sure he came tonight!"

She and Daphne were in the heated lobby of the rink, along with a few children and parents who'd evidently had a figure-skating lesson earlier. The bleachers were outside the lobby, rising up in a bank above the boxes where the players would sit.

"How tall is he?"

"Midrange."

"That rules out stumpy over there, and those two lumberjacks. I guess that's something."

"And he's not a goalie. Wait, is that—"

"You see him? Which one?"

"Shoot. I can't tell. I thought I saw him, but . . ."

"C'mon. We've got to go out there." Daphne headed for the glass door to the rink area.

"Daphne, wait! I can't go out there! He'll see me!"

"Pish. He will not."

"Daphne, there's no one else in the freakin' stands! Of course he'll notice!"

Daphne sat back down, a pout on her face. "Fine. We'll wait till the game starts. Then he'll be concentrating on it and won't look up."

Emma visored her hand over her forehead, half-hiding her face. "I knew I shouldn't have agreed to this."

"Look, we'll go up in the stands, we'll spot him, we'll watch the game, and then we'll tear out of here before it ends. Even if he thinks he sees you—which he won't—he won't be sure. You can always deny it if he asks."

"Lie to him? Yeah, great, that's what I want to do."

"Oh, stop making such a big deal out of this. There's no

crime in watching him play hockey. He'll probably be flattered. No one else has a hot babe in the stands."

Emma groaned.

A few minutes later, the players collected the extra pucks, and those on the first string took their positions. A puck was dropped between two players and a quick, furious battle of slapping blades knocked it away, with skaters in hot pursuit.

"Now!" Daphne said, bounding up and grabbing Emma by the sleeve, dragging her through the glass door.

Emma stumbled after her, the cold of the rink hitting her face. Only the boards and the Plexiglas panels of the rink were between them and the players now, and as the game shifted direction the herd of skaters turned. With scraping, running glides, their bodies hunched low, sticks wagging on the ice in front of them, they chased straight toward Emma and Daphne. Emma grabbed Daphne and hurried her toward the stands.

They had almost reached the shelter of a wall that hid the steps up to the stands when, glancing back over her shoulder, Emma saw one player look up at her and freeze. And although all she could see clearly were his eyes, she knew it was Russ.

The moment of distraction cost him dearly. Another skater hit him hard, sending him into the boards and glass right in front of Emma. The glass and frames shook, the impact sounding like it must have crushed half the bones in his body. Both skaters fell to the ice.

Emma dashed to the glass, pressing her hands and fore-head to it, trying to see down to the players.

"Was that him?" Daphne asked, appearing beside her.

Emma didn't answer, anxiously watching the skaters untangle themselves. One regained his feet, then put a hand out to help Russ up. Emma backed away from the glass as she saw him moving, no harm done.

He turned to her as soon as he was up, a question in his eyes. Another skater tapped him on the helmet with the handle of his stick and asked him a question Emma couldn't hear. A moment later, the skater looked at her and raised his hand.

"Hi, Emma!" he shouted, the sound barely coming through the glass.

Dumbfounded, she waved back.

The skater pointed to the stands.

Emma looked at Russ, who gave the faintest of shrugs and lifted his hand slightly, as if to say, "It's up to you." She couldn't tell if he was happy, angry, or indifferent.

Emma shrugged back, smiled in embarrassment, and headed for the stands with Daphne.

The game resumed, and when the players changed out Emma looked down at the box, picking out Russ. He was gesturing and talking to one of his teammates, and Emma had no idea what he was saying, although she guessed it related to the game rather than to her. Then two of the players farther down the line turned around and sought her out with their eyes.

"Hey, Emma! Come to see Buffy play?"

She smiled nervously and gave a little wave, not knowing how to respond.

"Buffy?" Daphne asked her softly.

Emma shrugged. "I've never heard it before."

Russ turned around and waved to her, and she wondered if it was a show for his friends. He wouldn't want to let on that he hadn't expected her, and might not want her here.

Unless they all knew of her "arrangement" with him?

The thought sent a chill down her back. He wouldn't have told them, would he? Down in the locker room, bragging about their prowess, he wouldn't have said anything about having a "kept woman," would he?

It would explain the amused friendliness of the players.

"Daphne, I think we should go."

"What? You've got to be kidding. This is great! And look, there goes Russ!"

Emma watched as he went out the gate and joined the play on the ice. Perhaps she'd stay for a minute more. She'd only seen snippets of hockey on TV and never been to a live game. They seemed to be wearing a pile of gear, and when they skated full speed she wondered at the strength and endurance it must take. Sticks slapped and the puck glided and she had no clue what was going on; she couldn't even tell where the puck was half the time. Russ was equally as hard to keep track of: the number of his jersey—12—wasn't always visible. Players changed in and out of the box, whistles blew for penalties she hadn't seen, and then suddenly the buzzer went off, stopping all play entirely.

"Do you have any clue what's going on?" Emma asked.

"Not a one."

"I think I've seen enough. We should go."

"Aw, come on. Stick it out. He knows you're here; he'll think it's weird if you bail on him now."

"I'm cold."

"So we'll get some hot chocolate out of the vending machines."

"Daphne—"

"What?"

"I—"

"*What?*"

"I don't know what Russ might have said about me. You know, locker-room talk. Everyone seemed a little too amused to see me."

Daphne frowned. "You think they know that you're fuck buddies?"

"Don't *call* it that! But yeah, I'm afraid they might know."

"Is Russ that kind of guy? One who would talk about it?"

Emma shrugged. "I don't really know. I don't *think* he would, but I don't know him beyond our nights together. I mean, people can be completely different in different situations, can't they?"

"Especially with sex as an incentive to be sweet, yeah." Daphne chewed her lip as the game restarted below. "Okay, here's what I think: your best bet is to stay here and meet those guys after they come out of the locker room."

"No! Absolutely not!" Emma's face flushed with heat, her stomach sinking.

"Hear me out. Right now, you're just a story they heard. *Assuming* they heard anything at all, and aren't just being friendly because they're friendly guys and are glad to have two hot babes like us watching their game."

Emma snorted.

"Hey, we're pretty good compared to the competition."

Emma raised a brow, looking pointedly around the empty stands.

"Exactly," Daphne said. "We're the only estrogen in the place. *But,* if Russ did tell them some sort of crap about you that he should have kept to himself, well, then that means he's not worth keeping. But it also means that if you meet the guys face-to-face and are charming and sweet, they'll like you and turn on Russ for being such a sleaze to you."

"Guys don't do that to each other."

"Sure they do. Some of them." She wrinkled her nose. "Maybe. But the point is, you can do more to save your reputation by meeting them than by slinking away."

"What do I care what my 'reputation' is with a bunch of men I've never met and will never see again?"

"If you don't care, then you shouldn't mind meeting them."

Emma scowled. "It doesn't work that way."

Daphne shrugged. "Then think of it this way: you don't know who those guys are. Russ is a rich entrepreneur. You don't know how many of those guys down there you really *might* meet again, as you make a name for yourself in architecture. Seattle's not that big a city, and there could be captains of industry down on that ice—doctors, lawyers, stockbrokers. Do you really want them to remember you as someone's booty on demand? Or do you want them to remember you as that incredibly nice and smart and funny woman that their asshole friend didn't treat as well as he should have?"

Emma thought for a long minute. Daphne was right. She could do more for herself by staying than by leaving. "Dammit."

A moment later number 12 slapped the puck, sending it sailing straight past the goalie and into the net. Emma leapt up and shouted, "Woo hoo! Way to go, Russ!"

He lifted his head at the sound, his mask turning toward her. He raised his stick in acknowledgment as a teammate slapped his back.

"See? You would have missed that!" Daphne said. "Got some quarters? I'll go get us some cocoa."

Emma watched the game, but her mind was wrapped up in the ordeal ahead. She was going to have to put on an Oscar-worthy performance to get through this evening. She would need divine inspiration if she was going to charm two teams of middle-aged hockey players.

*   *   *

What was she doing here? Russ wondered with a mix of anger and confusion as he showered after the game. Why had she come? What did she want?

No answer came to mind.

Of course, that was the problem between them: that sense he had that she had desires she wouldn't tell him. He would never have guessed she would do a thing like this.

He didn't like this kind of surprise, where he was left confused and uncertain as to motives. Though he'd felt a certain pleasure at knowing she was watching. James had watched a couple of his games, but no one else ever had.

He dried off and dressed quickly, taking part in the conversation around him with only half his attention until one of the guys, Frank, slapped him on the shoulder.

"Buffy, you dog! Here we all thought you were gay. Not that there's anything wrong with that! But jeez, no one remembers ever seeing a girlfriend of yours."

"You think I'd bring one to this place?"

Frank clamped his hand to his heart. "You wound me! You're ashamed of us?"

"Hey, you going to take her to Harold's?" Tom asked.

"That's cruel and unusual," Russ answered. "I don't want to scare her off."

"All serious girlfriends are required to spend one evening at Harold's," Frank said. "It's tradition."

"God knows they wouldn't want to spend a second," Russ said. "I don't think Emma would enjoy it."

"Of course she won't," Greg joined in, grinning. "Since when is that the point? Nope, she's got to come. Unless you don't intend her to be around for long?"

Russ tied his shoes, trying to keep his face impassive. He obviously couldn't explain why Emma didn't qualify for a Harold's initiation.

"You can't give her up!" Tom said. "Christ, she's gorgeous! You'll never get your hands on someone like that again!"

"I'm shocked he got a woman like that the first time," Frank said, standing with beer in hand, a towel wrapped around his hairy, pot-bellied waist. "After all, he doesn't have my hot body going for him."

Russ laughed and picked up his gear. "Yep, you've got a great twelve-pack."

Frank patted his gut. "Any woman would be proud to call this her own."

Russ headed out to the lobby, not knowing if Emma would still be there, but wanting to get to her before his teammates if she was. He had no idea what he would say to her; all he knew was that he had to get to her and find some answers.

Emma watched the Zamboni trundle around the ice and tried not to think about what Russ was going to say when he emerged from the locker room.

"I'll bet he's happy to see you," Daphne said, interrupting her determined oblivion. "You saw the way he raised his stick to you each time he scored. He was *glad* you were here."

"I don't know. Maybe he was just being polite. I was yelling his name, after all. His friends would have noticed if he'd ignored me."

"You worry too much. I'll bet he was flattered, and I'll bet you'll get some amazing sex out of it."

"I thought the point of this was to move beyond that."

"Not *beyond* it," Daphne said. "Just *in addition* to it."

Emma worried that she might have lost it completely with this stunt.

She heard a noise and turned.

Russ.

He set his bag and sticks down and came toward her, and there wasn't a smile on his face. Just an unsettling look of intensity. She couldn't tell what he was feeling, except that it was focused on her. She plastered a smile of greeting on her lips and hoped he didn't see the quavering uncertainty that she felt.

"Emma. I was surprised to see you came to the game."

"Russ! Yes, hi. Er . . . this is my friend Daphne."

Russ put out his hand and shook Daphne's. "It's a pleasure to meet you."

"It's nice to meet you, too." Daphne grinned at him with a little too much knowledge in her smile.

Russ scowled and turned to Emma. "Can we have a private word?"

"Go ahead!" Daphne said, and widened her eyes at Emma with an exaggerated "Ooh, you're in trouble!" expression.

"Yeah, sure," she said, and started to follow him. As she did so, though, a couple of guys emerged from the locker room and called out, "Emma! Watcha doing with a miserable old fart like Buffy, huh?"

She remembered what Daphne had said about doing her best to charm them, and gathered her courage. After a quick glance at Russ—who had frozen in place—she moved toward the men, extending her hand to shake theirs. "He's spry for his decrepit old age, and a young heart counts for a lot, don't you think? I'm Emma Mayson. It's a pleasure to meet some of Russ's teammates."

The men stared at her in shock for a moment, as if surprised that she could tease right back, then dropped their bags and shook her hand, introducing themselves as Frank and Tom.

"This is the first hockey game I've ever seen," Emma said, and decided to lay it on thick. "You all skate so fast!"

"Nah, we're slow," Frank said.

"You should see the guys who are nineteen, twenty," Tom said.

"You looked fast to me. I kept thinking how athletic you were, to move so well under all that equipment."

"Yeah, well . . ." Frank mumbled, and tilted his head. He almost looked ready to kick the ground, blush and say *Aw, shucks.*

"Let me introduce you to my friend Daphne Elliot. Daphne?" she called.

Daphne trotted over and Russ followed, looking cross at having lost control of the situation.

By the time she was finished introducing Daphne, more of Russ's teammates had emerged from the locker room and joined the group.

Emma tried to hide her shock. These guys were not guys; they were *men.*

Russ, at thirty-six, could easily be taken for five years younger than his age. Many of his teammates looked like they were well past forty and running fast toward fifty. Bald and balding, graying and gray, faces with the lines of wear, and bodies with the thickened waists of middle age. None were unattractive, but they all looked like people who would be friends with her mother, not with her. They were the guys who owned the repair shops and carpet stores; the ones who had filled your cavities since second grade and who came and fixed your refrigerator, and who tried to take a nap in the recliner while their kids wreaked havoc in the backyard.

They were adults, no matter how boyish they were acting now. She felt a floating sense of unreality, pretending that she fit in, in any way at all. She must appear a child to them.

"Hey, Russ, you played tonight like someone was watching, huh?" said a guy who introduced himself as Craig.

"Yeah, when was the last time you scored a goal?" Tom asked. "I don't even remember."

"Because I play right wing. I'm usually the one setting *you* up for goals."

"Two goals tonight!" Craig said, ignoring what he'd said to Tom. "You *definitely* knew someone was watching."

Emma turned wide-eyed to Russ, watching his reaction. There was a tensing in his jaw, and she wondered if it was embarrassment or anger. Had he really been showing off for her?

"You were a demon out there. Carrying the puck, making moves," Frank said, miming a skater on the ice. "You were *on*. You're never that aggressive, Buffy. Guess your balls knew Emma was in the stands and got woken up for once."

"Shut the hell up!"

Frank looked in pseudo-alarm at Emma and Daphne, his eyebrows high and mouth pursed. " 'Scuse the language!"

"Emma, Daphne, come with us to Harold's," Craig said.

"Harold's?" Emma asked.

"It's half a block away, a bar we all go to after the game to BS about how great we played."

Russ put his hand on her arm. "Emma, you'd hate it. You don't have to go."

"Don't listen to him!" Frank said. "The place is harmless.

We're harmless." He gestured at himself and at the others. "Harmless!"

Emma raised a brow, amused by the joshing of the men and trying to hide the tension between her and Russ. "I doubt you're completely harmless," she said. "But Daphne and I will come if you promise us one thing."

"Yeah?"

She glanced at Russ. "You have to tell us why you call Russ 'Buffy.' "

"Done!" Frank looked at Russ. "Don't worry, I won't make you look too big an idiot. Just moderately big."

"Hey, thanks," Russ said dryly.

"It was during his first year playing here at Aurora," Frank explained. "He wasn't used to this crap rink and got his stick jammed between the boards. The stick stopped and he kept going. Nearly impaled himself on it, like a suicidal vampire. Broke—what?—three ribs, was it, Buffy?"

"One."

"Let's call it two. So some smartass called him Buffy, like that vampire slayer chick."

"*You* called me it," Russ said.

Frank sighed fondly. "My kids used to love that show."

As people started heading for the exit, Russ grabbed his gear and walked with Emma and Daphne, pushing open the door into the cool night air and holding it for them. They waited while he loaded his stuff into his car; then the three of them walked through the amber-lit parking lot and over toward Harold's. Daphne drifted ahead a few steps.

"If you don't want me to go to Harold's, I won't," Emma said quietly.

"It's too late to change your mind. It would be worse if you left now."

"Do women usually come to Harold's?"

"Rarely. But don't let the guys intimidate you. They're mostly a good bunch, and the invitation is sincere. While they wouldn't want wives and girlfriends to show up all the time, they do enjoy a periodic appearance."

They were quiet for a few steps; then Emma gathered the courage to ask, "Are you angry with me?"

She saw him glance ahead at Daphne, who surely was listening with an eager ear. "Now is hardly the time to discuss it."

"I only meant to—"

"Hey, wait up!" someone called from behind them.

Damn.

She had the feeling this was going to be a very long evening.

Russ stood with his back against the bar and watched Emma and her friend at the table, surrounded by admirers.

Daphne didn't seem to be having any problem with an evening at Harold's. She was three seats away from Emma, talking to the only guy as young as Russ. Bob also happened to be single, and Russ dreaded that no matter what happened between him and Emma, Daphne might worm her way into the haven of his hockey family.

Emma had been the one to insist the nature of their relationship be kept strictly confidential. Had she broken that vow with her friend? The possibility sent an angry unease through him. It would be disastrous if Daphne knew and leaked that piece of gossip to Bob, and thus to everyone in the league.

There was solidarity among the hockey players, and a general live-and-let-live philosophy, but the line was drawn at lousy treatment of women. One guy who had cheated on his wife and brought his girlfriend to an out-of-town tournament had never been invited again, and had been frankly told not to bring his piece to Harold's. He didn't get invited to barbecues and picnics; no one wanted him and his mistress at their Christmas party or housewarming.

Russ had never thought that he might set himself up for that same ostracism.

Emma sucked the last of her diet Pepsi from the big plastic cup, the gurgling suction of her straw in the dregs all but lost beneath the noise of the bar. She glanced up, meeting his eyes. She looked childlike in that moment, big-eyed over her empty soda, surrounded by men larger and older than herself. Was she feeling uncomfortable under her facade of ease?

Next to her, Greg finished sketching his master suite on a napkin and pushed it toward her, drawing her attention.

"So this is what my wife wants to do. She wants to move this wall here, bump out the outer wall, and get both a walk-in closet and a 'spa bathroom' out of it, whatever that is. I keep telling her it won't work, that the spaces will be too tight and it'll be too expensive."

Emma bit her upper lip and stared at the crude drawing. From listening to her talk about design, Russ knew that she was forming the three-dimensional space in her mind, imagining it from different angles, putting herself inside it in the artificial reality of her imagination. He knew it was a mental exercise that took a unique, complex gift of intelligence, and when she concentrated like that, her gaze turned inward to the creative visions in her head, he found himself intensely attracted to her.

She was dressed more casually tonight than he was now used to seeing her. She was in jeans and hooded sweatshirt, her dark silky hair loose, nothing about her garb deliberately provocative, although he found the sight of her ass in jeans to be plenty of provocation. It occurred to him that this visit might have been an impulse on her part. Maybe she'd been in the neighborhood with her friend, and dropped into the rink on the chance that he might be playing.

It was disconcerting to see her outside her apartment, with a friend. Of course he knew that she had a life beyond her time with him; he just hadn't seen any of it.

"Here, show your wife this," Emma said, grabbing another napkin and Greg's pen. She quickly sketched out her idea, explaining the details as she went. "It's a more efficient use of space and should be less expensive to build, yet it should give a greater feeling of openness and of that luxury she wants."

Greg raised his brows, looking over the finished product. "Damn. I didn't want you to show me a way it would be possible; I wanted you to tell me I should spend my money on a boat instead."

She shrugged. "Sorry."

Greg turned around and waved the napkin at him. "Did you see her draw this? We can't let her and Tina get together. I'll be living in a remodel for the next ten years if they do."

Emma grinned. "In ten years it will be time to start all over again."

Greg turned to Russ and said in a stage whisper, "Keep those two apart. Far, far apart!"

He intended to, for completely different reasons. "Emma, would you like another soda?" he asked.

She looked at her watch, stifling a yawn. "No, it's past midnight. We ought to get going." She pushed back from the table and stood.

He stepped closer to her. "I'll follow you back to your place."

"I have to drive Daphne to her car. I won't be home until nearly one o'clock, I'm sure."

"I don't care if you're not home until five. I'm coming over."

She looked at him wide-eyed and he knew she was expecting an ugly scene. He didn't know how to reassure her with words, not when he didn't know how he felt, and not when there were half a dozen of his fellow players within earshot. Not knowing what else to do, he grabbed her hand and, out of sight of the others, squeezed it firmly. "I'll see you both to your car. It's not the type of neighborhood you should be walking around in on your own."

Emma nodded and pried Daphne away from her prey.

Greg got up at the same time. "I should have been home an hour ago," he said. "Tina will have my hide. I'll walk with you."

When Emma and Daphne were safely away in Emma's car, Greg put his arm over Russ's shoulder. "Now that, my fellow, was a sweet girl. Smart, too. You know I'm going to have to hurt you if you treat her badly."

"Does that mean I should keep seeing her, or break it off?" Russ replied.

Greg shoved the back of his head and headed for his own car. "She's a keeper, if you ask me. And I saw the way she looked at you."

"How did she look at me?"

"How do you think, you idiot?" Greg got in his car, slamming the door and leaving Russ to figure it out for himself.

Thirteen

W hat were you thinking?"

The words greeted her as she walked through the door to her apartment. Russ was already inside, which didn't surprise her since she had dawdled on her return here, dreading facing him.

"I wanted to see you play," she said, setting her purse down on the end of the breakfast bar. He was standing in the center of her living area, hands on hips.

"Why?"

She shrugged, trying to think of an excuse. The last thing she would tell him that her interest in him was growing well beyond the sexual. "Curiosity. I don't know anything about hockey except what you've told me."

"You could have looked it up online or bought a book. Why did you come to my game? I didn't even mention it to you."

"But you play the same place every week. Your team's schedule is on the Internet."

His eyes widened slightly. "You looked it up?"

"I was curious, that's all! I wanted to see you play, and I didn't think you'd want me to watch. My intention was that you not see me at all. How was I to know that no one else watches the games, and Daphne and I would stick out like palm trees on the polar ice cap?"

"So you planned to conceal it from me."

Her apprehensions of the evening slipped over into anger and she raised her voice. "I didn't *plan* to do anything! And what's the big deal, anyway? Huh? You sleep with me three times a week; it doesn't seem such a crime that I want to learn a little bit more about you!"

"*Is* that what you want? To know more about me?"

"It feels like you know all there is to know about me, but you give me precious little insight into your own life."

"I've shared more with you than I have with anyone in the past five years."

She tucked in her chin, taken aback. She hadn't expected that. "Are you serious?"

"It's not something I'd lie about."

She frowned, trying to figure him out. "Why me? Why tell me so much?"

"Maybe because you tell me so little."

"What are you talking about?" she asked, stunned. "You know everything."

"I don't know how to please you in bed."

The statement took the breath from her, guilt sweeping over her. "I'm happy with how you treat me in bed."

He shook his head. "You know what I'm talking about, Emma. You won't let me give to you the same pleasure that you give to me. Why?"

"Because this isn't about me. This whole relationship is about pleasing you. That's my job."

"Maybe I don't want to feel like you're doing me as your job."

"You seemed happy enough!"

"Even a kid will get sick of candy eventually and want something real to eat."

She felt stricken. "You're sick of me?"

He came forward and held her by the shoulders. "I'm not sick of you. Nor am I some stereotyped horndog who cares only about himself. I want to make love to the real Emma, not a French servant girl or a harem wench. Not even to someone whose mind is elsewhere, and whose only goal is to get me off. There is pleasure in giving pleasure: pleasure in knowing that you've touched a place deep inside a person; that she's trusted you with her secret desires, and felt safe enough to lose control in your arms. You've deprived me of that—whether by design or ignorance or fear, I don't know. But without it, we can't go on."

"I like what you do to me, Russ—truly I do. I don't know why I don't stay with it all the way; why I don't let you get me 'there.'"

He slid his hand up her neck and into her hair. "What am I doing wrong? Why won't you open up to me?"

"I don't even open up to myself," she said softly.

"Why?"

She leaned forward, resting her forehead against his chest. "I don't know. I think I'm afraid."

"Of what?" he asked more gently.

"Of embarrassing myself. Making a fool of myself. Being laughed at. Being vulnerable."

She felt him smooth his hand through her hair. "It's okay to be afraid. It's not okay to let that fear stifle you." He kissed her temple, his lips lingering as he whispered, "Tell me what you want."

His words shivered down her spine and she closed her eyes. "I don't know what I want."

He stepped back, holding her away from him. She opened her eyes in surprise.

"You have to tell me, Emma. Tell me what you want me to do to you. Spell it out in English."

She hunched her shoulders, the thought of telling him where and how to touch her too mortifying to accept. "I can't do that."

He dropped his hands. "I can't continue like this. We're finished, then."

Panic flashed through her. "No!"

"It's your choice."

"But— But you can't mean that I have to verbally guide you to my own orgasm!"

He picked his jacket up off the couch. "You can stay in the apartment as long as you need to."

"No! Russ, wait!"

He held still, watching her.

"Wait. I . . ." She couldn't speak. Couldn't do this thing he wanted of her.

He moved toward the door.

"I want you to put your coat down!"

He turned, cocking an eyebrow at her.

"And . . . and then I want you to pick me up and carry me to the bedroom!"

He draped his jacket over the breakfast bar and came toward her. Alarm ran up her spine and she was filled with sudden apprehension. They'd been intimate for weeks, but an embarrassed modesty swept over her as he approached. This would be the first time that the focus was all on her. He was putting the control of what happened in her hands, but only so that she would reach a point where she lost her grip on it completely.

She was being forced to give him the keys to her surrender. She was being forced to admit there were things she wanted that only he could give her.

He swept her up in his arms, surprising a gasp from her as she found herself lifted off her feet. She wrapped her arms around his neck as he carried her toward the bed-room.

"What if I can't, you know—*get there*?" she asked, a qua-ver in her voice.

"Have you ever managed to in the past?"

She nodded.

"Then you can't use that as an excuse." He pushed open the door and used his elbow to flip on the light. "Now what?"

"You mean I have to keep telling you things until I feel *it*?" The thought flitted through her mind that she could pretend to reach the big O and he might not know.

"I've said what I expect." He raised a brow. "And don't think I can't tell if you're faking."

She sighed. "I guess we should get this over with, then."

"Such passion!"

"How am I suppose to feel lusty on demand?" she asked querulously.

He shifted her in his arms, her weight obviously begin-ning to drag on him. "You've managed it for several weeks."

It was true. She knew that she only needed to consciously decide to accept the situation. She might not always be in the mood when he visited, but if she went ahead with foreplay and sex anyway, she almost always ended up enjoying it; or at least not disliking it. Sometimes she'd enjoyed it most when she'd initially thought she'd rather be reading a book.

This, though, was different. This time she had to fully en-gage both body and mind. Orgasms never happened while thinking about anything other than one's own pleasure. Was it really okay to be so selfish?

She realized he was waiting for his next command. "You can put me down."

"On the bed?"

"No, let me stand."

He set her down and she straightened her clothes. So, here they were in her brightly lit bedroom. What now? "Okay, um . . . I guess I should tell you to seduce me."

He shook his head. "You'll have to be more specific than that."

"Er, how about, 'Let's get naked and in bed and then you will, uh, stimulate me to the point of orgasm.' " Her cheeks colored. *Stimulate,* ugh, what a word.

He shook his head again. "Step by step, Emma. Every touch, every motion."

She chewed her upper lip, nervousness making her hands tremble as she went around the room and lit the candles, aware of him watching her every move. She flipped off the overhead light, then turned to him, her hands twisted together. "This isn't going to be much fun for you, is it?"

A wicked smile pulled at the corner of his mouth. He looked different in the darkened room, his face harder, less knowable, his eyes shadowed but for a glimmer of reflection from the candlelight. "Won't it?"

A shiver breezed across her skin, sending ripples of anticipation through her. She hadn't ever seen Russ like this, an undertone of angry frustration coloring his desire. It alarmed her, even as it touched something deep inside her.

He cared enough to be angry that she kept part of herself closed away from him. He cared enough to try to change it, instead of just leaving. If she hadn't sensed that his caring was at the heart of this, she would've let him go. Knowing he cared helped a little bit.

"Okay, um . . . I suppose you should get undressed." She mentally rifled through the sexual scenarios in her books, searching for something to use, but her books had focused on pleasing a man, not on pleasing herself. That was something she did alone.

Russ's shirt and shoes were off in the space of moments. My, he was an efficient follower of commands.

A devil of mischief roused inside her. "Slowly," she said. "And make it sexy." She sat down on the edge of the bed to watch the show.

Russ lowered his hands slowly to his belt buckle and started to undo it. He rocked his hips from side to side, dancing to an off-tempo rhythm in his own mind.

Emma covered her lips with her fingertips, hiding her smile. The big sweetie couldn't dance.

The buckle undone, he whipped the belt out of the loops in one long pull and then cracked his belt like a whip.

Emma yelped as the end of it hit her dresser, knocking over a candle.

"Crap!" Russ said, quickly righting the burning candle.

Emma slid her hand over her face, giggling and peering at him through her fingers.

Russ tossed the belt aside and returned to the center of the room with a shrug. He began to sing under his breath to the traditional burlesque strip tease theme, "Dah DOOP dah dah, dah DOOP dah dah, dah DOOP dah DAAH daah," as he unbuttoned his pants and pulled down the zipper.

Despite her laughter, Emma found herself watching that zipper go down. Just as he started to part the front of his pants he turned around, his butt to her.

Ass-shaking followed as he lowered his pants, revealing black Jockeys over that rounded skater's tush that she had admired from the beginning. His thighs and calves were dusted with dark hair.

He let the pants drop to his ankles, the tops of his socks peering out above the crumpled material. He tried to step out of his pants but his feet got caught up in them, a pant leg turning inside out as it clung to his sock-clad foot. He stumbled, then bent down to free his foot. He peered past his knee at her while he was down there and saw her watching. He narrowed his eyes, and then his face disappeared on the other side of his legs and he started to do a butt dance, bobbing it up and down, side to side.

Emma laughed out loud, the spectacle of his dancing tush above the socks and tangled trousers too much to take.

Then his hands came up and his thumbs looped into the

elastic of his Jockeys. He inched them down, the crack of his ass appearing.

"No, no!" Emma laughed.

He stood up straight, thumbs still in his half-lowered Jockeys, and looked over his shoulder at her. "Oh yeah, baby!"

Emma fell over on her side. "Stop! My stomach hurts!"

He stopped dancing and turned around, walking toward her with his underpants stuck awkwardly over his erection, the trousers dragging behind him. "Your wish is my command."

Emma rolled onto her back and covered her eyes with her arm. "Just, just . . . take it all off, will you?"

His dance had broken some of the tension, making her forget for a moment how serious this all was to him.

"All right," he said softly. "What do you want me to do, Emma?"

She closed her eyes. What did she want? What could she ask him to do that would guarantee excitement and orgasm?

It was too much pressure.

"I don't know," she said. "I don't know what will get me there."

"Forget about that. Start with where we are now. Look at me."

She opened her eyes, turning her head to look at him.

Lord, he was gorgeous. The candlelight licked gently at his skin, shadowing the definition of muscles in chest, arms, abdomen. His thighs were thick and strong, and his erection rose firmly from an unfathomable abyss of dark hair. Her gaze skimmed up his body to his face.

He was gorgeous, her own dark god come to please her. A month ago she would have given a year off her life to have an opportunity like this. It would be pitiful if she couldn't think of at least one thing she'd like him to do to her. Not putting a gorgeous, willing man to good use was one regret she didn't want to have.

"Could you touch me here?" she asked tentatively, raising her shirt and hoody and pointing to her belly.

Russ knelt down beside the bed. "Here?" He lay his palm on her skin.

"Yes."

He stroked his hand lightly over her, his touch gentle. His touch circled, tracing a wider route, drifting down over her sides and up to the edge of her shirt and the waist of her low-cut jeans. Emma closed her eyes, his gentle stroking both relaxing and arousing. It reminded her how much they had already shared together, and that she had no reason not to trust him.

Each time his hand stroked up toward her shirt, she wished it would go higher; he seemed to be teasing her with the possibility. He didn't go any farther, though, even when she moved so that her breasts would be closer to his hand.

She opened her eyes and looked at him, moving again so that her message was clear.

The wicked smile returned to his lips. "You have to tell me. Say it out loud."

"You know what I want."

"Say it."

"Are you getting off on this?" she complained.

The wicked grin widened. "Yeah, I am."

The admission sent a tremor through her. "Really?"

He moved his hand slowly across her belly, the edge of his fingers skimming the waistband of her jeans, sending a shiver straight down her panties. "Yes," he said, "I really am enjoying this."

"I don't want to disappoint you," she admitted.

He sighed. "The only way you'll disappoint me is if you lie there worrying about what I'm thinking. Be selfish. Be rude. Be crass and ask for raunchy things that you think will revolt me. Ask for silly things. Embarrassing things!"

"Why is it so hard to do?" she asked softly.

"Maybe because you've never done it."

She lay her hand over his on her stomach, holding his large, strong hand still. He was right: she'd never done it, not with anything in her life. The realization had been growing in her since meeting Russ; it had been appearing to her repeatedly in different forms, but the theme was the same in each go-round. She'd seen it enough now to be heartily sick of it.

If she couldn't find and ask for what she, Emma Mayson, wanted in a situation as safe and enticing as this one, then she might as well give up on ever achieving any of her dreams. A life of utter mediocrity and disappointment was all she'd ever have.

"Undo my jeans," she said. "Take them off."

He did as she asked, his fingers hard against her soft flesh as he struggled with the button. She felt a smile pulling at her mouth.

"You're not used to being the seducer, are you?" she asked.

He fought the button free and made short work of her zipper. "I'm a quick learner." He nudged her to lift her hips, and a moment later her jeans were gone, her shoes going with them.

"Socks," she said. "Off. Then . . ." she hesitated. She wanted it, but she couldn't imagine he'd want to do it. She herself wouldn't want to do it to him.

He peeled her socks off. "What do you want?"

"Could you . . ."

"Tell me."

"Suck my toes? Lick my arch?"

He laughed and climbed up onto the bed, sitting near her feet. He seemed completely unselfconscious of his nakedness, although sitting tailor fashion left his goodies in plain sight. Holding her heel in the palm of his hand, he met her eyes and raised her foot toward his mouth.

Emma laughed nervously and covered her eyes with her hands. Her toes curled in anticipation, and she was embarrassingly aware that with her leg raised and her panties off, she was giving him just as big a display as he was giving her.

He kissed the side of her foot where the arch began its curve, then darted his tongue out in a quick flick.

It tickled more than anything. "Harder," she said, peering between her fingers.

He ran the point of his tongue against her arch, apparently as hard as he could. Emma flinched and laughed. "No, that tickles!"

He did it again and again, and she tried to get away, her hands coming down to push against the mattress. She tugged her foot, but he held tight and licked.

"No, not like that!" Laughter made her weak, helpless under his torture.

Russ relented and did as he knew she wanted, using the flat of his tongue to stroke her arch. He'd only tickled her to get her to relax, just as he'd deliberately fumbled the striptease.

He had thought, given Emma's bold sexual adventuring, that she'd deliberately kept from opening up to him. Instead, she was just as shy in her way as he was in his. Maybe even more so; at least he had ten years' more experience with expressing his wants in bed, however hesitant those expressions might be.

That she was trying to open up to him now meant a lot to him; he did not underestimate the fragility of the trust she was offering him. Whatever she wanted, he would do it and be grateful she had shared it with him.

At the end of this night, she would have no physical secrets left. The thought of feeling her contractions around him as he thrust deep inside; of seeing her face lost in passion he had created; of knowing she had given herself over to him completely: it made him hard, and he knew he would stay that way through any length of toe sucking.

Before Emma, he hadn't spared more than a passing thought for what went on below the surface of a woman's mind. He hadn't cared enough to ask, and hadn't understood how much it could mean to him.

In his youth, he hadn't even suspected that a woman might hold part of herself separate, that what he saw wasn't all there was to get.

He licked the arch of her foot again and she squirmed, her hands fisting at her sides. She had closed her eyes, and despite the fact that she was dictating his actions, he felt more in control than he ever had with her. It was hard to beat the thrill of a woman writhing in pleasure under his touch.

He looked at her pristine toes and did as she had asked, one toe at a time. He dipped his tongue between each one as he sucked, rubbing against the tender skin. Emma bared her teeth as if in pain and her whole body tensed. She held perfectly still, as if afraid that moving would stop what he was doing.

He would never have guessed her toes were an erogenous zone.

He did the last of her toes and set her foot down.

She rolled onto her stomach and he admired her rounded behind before she twisted and sat up, her back still to him. She peered over her shoulder at him. "Finish undressing me."

He put his hands on her hips and slid his palms up her

sides, her T-shirt and hoody coming with them. She raised her arms as he moved upward, then detoured to her breasts, brushing his palms over the mounds pressing into the silky stretch material of her bra. He circled there until he felt her nipples hardening, making pebbles beneath the material.

He pulled her tops off and tossed them onto the floor, then turned his attention to her one remaining garment.

He cupped her breasts in his hands, thumbs stroking over their peaks, then slid his hands back toward her sides and forward again, this time his fingers inside the material. He ran her nipples between his fingers, pinching them gently, and leaned forward until his lips were just above the nape of her neck.

He could hear her breath from her parted lips, and he wanted to lay his mouth against her skin. He waited for her to ask him to, and when she didn't, that stretch of naked skin became twice the temptation. He raised his mouth beside her ear, knowing that she could feel the heat of his breath.

He gently withdrew his hands from her bra and unfastened it, easing the straps down over her shoulders and pulling her back against him as he skimmed over her breasts in a touch that was more tease than caress, taking the lingerie with him. It joined the rest of their clothes on the floor.

"Play with my breasts," Emma said softly.

A command with which he was happy to comply. He

held them tenderly in his palms and she rested her head against the crook of his neck and relaxed, her hands resting on his thighs. He could see down the slope of her chest to her breast in his hand. He gently squeezed, then massaged, watching as they changed shape under his touch, his excitement rising as he saw his hands on her nude breast, her nipple appearing between his fingers, vulnerable to his play. He traced around her aureole, then grasped the nipple between several fingertips and slowly, gently pulled outward, as if her nipple were a sucker being pulled from a mouth.

"Go lower," Emma whispered.

He slid his hands down her torso, then back up again, and felt goose bumps rise on her skin.

"Lower."

He skimmed the base of her abdomen, fingertips barely touching the beginning of her nether hair.

"Lower."

He trailed his fingertips down over the tops of her thighs, returning upward on their soft inner sides only to repeat the same path again. Emma parted her legs in invitation and he skimmed up to, but not touching, her sex.

He wanted to touch it; wanted to feel if she was damp for him yet; if her entrance pulsed for him. He wanted to feel her warm soft inner lips part for him, and to feel her arch her hips against his hand.

But she had to ask for it.

She seemed to have forgotten the necessity of words. She

parted her legs yet farther and reached up and back with one hand to hold his neck.

The sides of his index fingers met where leg curved into sex, his thumbs touching the surface of her curls but no deeper. He pressed his hands harder against the inner tops of her thighs, massaging in a circle, knowing that the motion would transfer to her sex.

Emma pulled away from him, leaving his hands and arms empty. She peered over her shoulder at him, then lay down on her stomach, stretching across the bed.

"Massage the backs of my thighs and my backside. Please." She tucked her face into her arm, lifting her head again a moment later to peer at him over her arm, as if uncertain whether she'd asked too much.

Hardly.

He went to work on her thighs and buttocks, although his hands yearned to tease her until she whimpered *Now. Take me, now.* But as he rubbed her thigh Emma gave a soft *mmm* of pleasure, and he realized that her erogenous zones weren't limited to her toes, breasts, and her sex. Her whole body wanted to be touched, caressed, made love to by his hands.

He felt a fool for having missed that fact in all the times they'd been together. He'd been touching her the way *he* wanted to be touched, hands diving right for the goods, forgetting that a woman's approach to sensuality could be different entirely.

It was going to be torture for his eager body. Each *ooh* and *ahh* and *mmm* she made as he massaged the backs of her legs and her buttocks went straight to his crotch. He wanted to hear her make those noises as he parted her thighs and pressed the head of his cock against her, her slit parting under him, the wet, hot slickness of her passage tight against him as he slid deep inside. He could already feel himself there, his hands on her hips as she pushed back against him, writhing and moaning with the pleasure he brought her.

Christ. He was going to have to think of lust-killing things like tax forms to make it through this.

But what sweet torture.

Emma felt his hands moving on her as she had asked and tried to relax and enjoy it. She knew now that he would continue this as long as she wanted, but she sensed a hint of impatience in his touch.

He was the one who had insisted on doing as she wished despite her embarrassment: he could suffer for it.

The thought that she was subtly torturing him was perversely freeing. She could revel in that, in a way that she was afraid to revel in asking for what she wanted without thought of his own pleasure.

One of his massaging hands slipped between her thighs and pressed a little too close to her sex, setting off a shiver of sensation. It was deliciously tempting, but she wasn't going to give in to it. Not yet.

"My lower back," she ordered, and made a small *mmm* of pleasure when he obeyed. Her skin seemed to soak up each touch of his hands, the very act of contact changing something within her. She was aroused and relaxed at the same time, an intoxicating, shimmering pleasure moving through her blood, drugging her, making her feel that she could continue like this forever. She wanted him to touch every part of her, from back to shoulders to the tender inner bend of her arm, to the sensitive center of her palm. She gave voice to her wishes, sending him on a treasure hunt over her body, finding the places that had lain undiscovered through all their joinings.

It was only when he'd touched every inch of her except her sex; only after he'd gently stroked her eyebrows and the shape of her ears; after he'd run the flats of his hands down the front of her torso, treating her breasts as any other part of her body, making her stretch her arms above her head and arch her back in catlike contentment; only after he'd touched the smooth space behind her ear and let his fingertips press over the faint ridges of her rib cage, that she knew she was ready to ask for something more.

"Lie on top of me and kiss me. I want to feel trapped. Pinned."

She felt his weight on her, his arousal a hard thickness against her loins. "Now kiss me like you're starving for it, and won't take no for an answer."

"No problem," he murmured, and took her face between

his hands. His eyes looked down into hers with dark intensity, almost animal in their naked hunger.

She closed her eyes and let him kiss her, enjoying the sure, hungry movements of his mouth on hers and the weight of his body. She *wanted* to be ravished, to be taken without permission by him, if only within the confines of this game they were playing tonight.

She wrapped her arms around his chest and one leg around the back of his. "Take me," she whispered against his ear as his mouth sucked at the edge of her jaw. "Now." She moved her hips against his erection, feeling it slide against her mound, his position changing enough that the head ran down her sex and across her slick wetness.

"Tell me how," he growled into her ear. "Spell it out, Emma."

She felt the head rubbing against her opening, teasing at her with its blunt hardness that refused to enter. "Don't ask. Just do it. That's what I want!"

"Say it. Say how."

Frustration boiled up within her and in a flurry of motion she fought out of his embrace, making him yelp in surprise and climb off her. She rolled onto all fours, looked over her shoulder at him, moved her knees apart and lowered her torso, her sex spread out in an unmistakable target. "Is *this* clear enough for you?"

Without another word he put one hand hard on her hip and the other to his cock for guidance, and she gasped as he thrust inside her with one long, deep stroke. She dropped her forehead down onto the mattress, feeling him move the length of her, stroking hard, his thickness within her body and seeming to take up half of it. She was no longer in sole possession of her body, and it was just what she wanted.

"Your fingertip," she gasped out in near incoherence, wanting him to reach around and stroke her nub.

"What was that?"

"Your finger. Use your finger."

There was a pause; then she felt his hands on her buttocks. Her eyes widened, but before she could stop him she felt the tip of one finger dip into her back door.

Shock held her motionless.

His thrusts resumed their former energy, his fingertip following the rhythm, pressing in and releasing along with each thrust.

Her psyche was overwhelmed by the double penetration, the double possession. A cool liquid rush washed over her, and she lost all sense of where she ended and he began.

With her right hand she reached down to her sex, touching the joining of their bodies, feeling the wetness and the movement of flesh against flesh. Her fingertips damp, she trailed them to her nub and stroked.

Triple contact now, her whole consciousness existing in the trio of sensations. They blended together, amplifying each other: thrusts of his cock inside her, the pressure of his fingertip at her back opening, the tingling pleasures of her own hand at work on her desire.

Ohh God, it felt so good . . .

She felt herself rising on the tide, felt the tension in her body as she strained toward the crest of the wave.

Yes, yes, it's coming, it's coming . . .

Her body tensed, her lower legs clamping against his thighs, a high-pitched keen vibrating in her throat. She held for a moment at the crest of the wave, balanced there, precarious, and then with one more stroke of his cock she felt herself tumble down the slope. Her inner muscles clenched around him, squeezing and releasing rapidly.

"Oh God, Emma," Russ groaned, and thrust once more deep inside her, where she felt the pulses of his own release blend with hers.

Emma closed her eyes in the afterglow. She felt Russ rest lightly upon her with his cock still deep inside, breathing heavily.

She carefully lay flat and then he rolled them both to their sides, spooned together. She felt him nuzzle his face into her hair.

A smile curled on her lips and she fell into slumber, their bodies still one.

In the bathroom a half hour later, washing up together, Russ glanced at Emma. She caught his look and smiled, a sleepy cat-contented smile. She stood on tiptoe and kissed his cheek.

"Thank you," she whispered.

"What wouldn't I do to please you?" he asked softly, the words a question for himself as much as her.

"I wouldn't mind finding out," she said, and laughed.

Russ smiled, and felt his own cowardice. He had asked her what she wanted him to do to her body, but he hadn't had the nerve to ask her the more important question: What did she want from him when it came to her heart?

It was a question he likely would never have the chance to ask. It wouldn't be fair, when he was paying her; he wouldn't put her in the position of having to pretend to be in love with him in order to keep her "job."

"Don't take too long," she said, patting his buttocks as she left the bathroom.

He watched her go, then looked at himself in the mirror. What had he become?

He was a permanent john, buying sex in lieu of the love that every man craved, whether he admitted it or not, whether he realized it or not.

He had become a man falling in love with the woman he had turned into a mistress. The woman he had, through his own actions, put beyond his reach for anything more than what was physical.

"Russ?" Emma called softly. "Are you coming back to bed?"

He turned away from the mirror and shut off the light, and returned to the soft comfort of Emma's body.

Fourteen

Emma cruised down the freeway, the stiff shocks of her Honda jouncing her with each rut and ripple in the road. She didn't care. Nor did she care about the red Porsche that seemed to find her car a direct challenge to its manhood, passing her with deliberate, finger-flipping speed.

She was lost in the memories of the night with Russ. Again she felt his hands on her inner thighs from behind, parting her, his fingertips reaching to her center to stroke her gently and then delicately parting her inner opening and laying the head of his rod against her. She felt him easing himself into her in slow, shallow thrusts, angled to hit her G-spot. She felt again his fingertip going where she'd least expected.

Her inner muscles clenched in memory of the orgasm that followed.

Even better had been the wash of relief that had flooded

through her, as if she had set down an immense burden. No more holding back, no more putting her own desires secondary, no more keeping her wishes secret from him, as if asking him to touch her *here* or *there* was too big a demand. She had opened herself completely to him. She had surrendered to her own desires, confessing wishes she hadn't even known she had.

And it was glorious.

Euphoria shimmered through her body, the whole world golden and filled with possibility this morning. Her mind floated free, random images of Russ and the landscape around her filling her head.

As if from a source beyond herself, an image began to form in her mind, composed of the streaming sunlight and tall dark firs around her. Planes and angles appeared, mimicking where sky met water and water met the upward thrust of a rocky, fir-covered island. Graceful curves swirled through it, like the cupped sail of a boat, the beat of a bird's wing. They became ramps easy to drive upon, easy to walk upon. And at the bottom edge of this growing vision were the multiple hatched lines of sandpiper tracks on the sand, becoming train tracks cutting through the station.

Excitement coursed through her and she traced over the building that was forming shape in her mind, solidifying it in her memory, adding details to cement it into place. She captured it wall by ramp by window, ensuring that it would still be with her later.

This was it! This was finally it! A vision of pure imagination that would be the train station she would want to visit, that she would want to welcome people to her city, that would be her vision of Seattle and the region.

It would unquestionably be too expensive to build; probably impossible from a structural standpoint. It was completely impractical.

And she didn't care. It was what she wanted. *She*, Emma Mayson.

Ahead, the Porsche had zipped into the right-hand lane and been trapped behind a semitruck, a poky RV on its left locking it in fume-sucking position. Coming up behind the RV, Emma moved into the passing lane to get by. As she moved past the RV, a space opened up between the RV and the semi and the Porsche shot in front of the RV with barely a foot to spare, causing the RV to rock on its shocks as the driver overreacted in surprise.

What type of asshole was driving that penis car?

The red Porsche gave a single flash of the turn signal and pulled forward, barely enough to get ahead of Emma. The jerkwad was going to cut her off!

Before she knew it, Emma's hand found the red button to the nitrous system of the street-racing Honda and her rebellious thumb hit the button. A moment later she was on the space shuttle, rocketing forward in a roaring burst of speed that knocked her head back against the headrest. Her wild scream of glee echoed in her head, drowning out the motor.

The Porsche disappeared in her rearview mirror, and she screamed all the way to her exit, a mile later. She drifted up the exit ramp to the light, the car now surprisingly docile in her control, as if it finally understood who was boss. A cool flush of receding adrenaline loosened her muscles.

She was still sitting in dreamy contentment at the light when something red moved up beside her. She turned her head and saw the Porsche in the lane on her left, waiting to go the opposite direction. Still buoyed by confidence, Emma rolled down her tinted window, letting the bastard who was driving see the girl who'd just whupped his ass.

As her window lowered, the driver of the penis car lowered his. With a smirk of satisfaction, Emma looked into the Porsche.

And saw a ponytailed blonde, not much older than her, who was looking at Emma with the same surprised embarrassment that Emma felt. They were women, behaving like asshole guys. In unison they turned away from each other, windows going back up to hide their shame.

Emma looked up at the light and willed it to turn green, fingers clenched on the steering wheel. When it finally did, the Honda and Porsche made their turns with ladylike decorum and headed off in opposite directions, well under the speed limit.

Fifteen

H ow many cloves of garlic?" Russ asked.
"Three."

"They're worse to peel than onions. The skins keep sticking to my fingers." He held up hands covered in white shreds.

Emma laughed and took the clove from him. "I'll show you a trick." They'd started cooking together a month ago, after her creative breakthrough about the train station. She'd had only two weeks to put her idea on a foam poster board before the deadline. When Russ had seen how frantically she was working to get it done, he'd volunteered to do the cooking.

One awful meal was enough to persuade Emma that a better solution was to e-mail him a grocery list; then, when he arrived at the apartment with the food, to prepare the meal with him as her sous-chef. It would have been simpler to buy takeout, but she enjoyed working side by side with him.

Over the past month an easy familiarity had grown between them; a comfort that hadn't been there before that night at the hockey rink. It felt as if a few of the walls between them had been removed. They cuddled up on the futon couch to watch *The Daily Show* or *Letterman* together some nights, and on Fridays he stayed until dawn, his arm over her as they slept spooned together.

But they hadn't again gone out together in public.

Emma set the clove of garlic on the cutting board, put the flat of her chef's knife over it, and gave the blade a solid whack with the heel of her hand.

"Careful!" Russ warned.

"Look." She held up the clove, now fissured and easily rid of its skin.

Her cell phone started ringing before Russ could respond to her culinary feat. She looked over at the phone, her heart tripping.

Russ raised a brow, understanding in his eyes. "Are you going to answer?"

Emma wiped her hands on a dish towel and went to the phone. It was now two weeks since she'd turned in her design, and today was the day that the finalists in the train station contest were to be notified. She'd been waiting for a call all day, pacing her apartment and staring out the window.

She picked up the phone with a shaking hand and looked at the display.

"Is it them?" Russ asked.

"I don't know. I don't recognize the name or number." She flipped open the phone and put it to her ear. "Hello?" she croaked.

"Hello! This is Mavis Hunter from the City of Seattle's Planning and Development Office. I'm trying to reach Emma Mayson."

"This is she." Emma met Russ's eyes and nodded, her own eyes wide and her heart kerthumping in her chest.

"Ms. Mayson, I'm pleased to tell you that you are one of the ten finalists in the King Street Station design competition. Congratulations!"

An *"eep"* escaped Emma's throat and the phone slid out of her hand, landing on the floor. Emma followed it down, sinking gracelessly into a sprawled sitting position.

"Ms. Mayson? Ms. Mayson?" the voice called tinnily from the phone.

Emma looked up at Russ and blinked. *"Meeep!"*

"Emma?" Russ said.

"Ms. Mayson?" the phone queried.

She managed a tight, fractional nod of her head.

"You got it?" Russ asked.

She nodded.

Russ scooped up the phone as he sat beside Emma and pulled her close. "Hi. Emma is too happy to speak at the moment, I'm afraid."

Emma heard the woman laugh and start talking again.

She reached for the phone and Russ gave it back. "I'm here!" she squeaked out. "I'm okay, I'm here!"

Mavis explained what would happen next and what Emma would need to do. Afraid that she wouldn't remember a word of it the moment she hung up the phone, Emma walked on her knees to her desk, reaching for a notepad and pen.

"Okay, so that was what time again?" Emma asked, writing down the information. When the call ended she closed the phone and looked up at Russ.

"You're a finalist?"

She smiled with her lips closed, the expression of happiness tentative, as if she couldn't quite believe it. She was still too stunned to take it in and react with the joy she had expected.

Russ did it for her. "Emma, that's wonderful! Congratulations!" He pulled her up off the floor and embraced her in a bear hug, lifting her off her feet and spinning in a circle.

She laughed, his enthusiasm taking her by surprise.

He planted a big kiss on her cheek. "I'm so proud of you, honey."

The "honey" took her by surprise, too. He'd never used a pet name with her before. She met his eyes, wondering what it meant, but he didn't seem to know he'd said anything of significance. If it was significant.

"You're on your way, Emma! Someone has finally noticed your brilliance!"

"Hardly! I'm just a finalist," she said, self-doubt snaking into her nascent joy. "There were probably only ten entries."

"Don't discount your achievement. This means something, Emma. Be proud of it! We need to celebrate: I should go get a bottle of champagne."

"Sure. That would be nice," Emma said with little enthusiasm. When he'd said they should celebrate, she'd gotten a sudden image of them going out to dinner, maybe someplace elegant and celebratory like the ultraposh restaurant Canlis. "You wouldn't want to go out?" she asked tentatively.

"After peeling all that garlic? Dinner's already half-made! The fish won't keep, will it?"

She couldn't tell if he was genuinely concerned, or if it was a way to get out of going out in public with her. She had no right to expect him to take her out; that had never been part of their arrangement. She had to remember that they weren't in a real relationship. Which made it difficult to ask the favor she wanted to request now.

"The fish would keep, but you're right, dinner is half-made. I'll finish up if you want to run out for the champagne."

"Great!" He reached for his coat and then paused, watching her as she went into the kitchen and focused on chopping garlic, not looking his way. "This is okay with you, isn't it?"

She looked up at him and gave him a big smile. "Yes! Of course!"

"Are you sure?"

"Yes!" She smiled too brightly, the corners of her mouth aching.

He frowned. "I want this to be special for you. Would you rather I stayed and helped with dinner? Or finished it myself? Why don't I do that, and you can sit and have a glass of wine."

He obviously had no idea of what she was thinking, and she wasn't going to enlighten him. But perhaps this would be as good a time as any to make another request. "There is a favor I wanted to ask you," she began tentatively.

He put down his coat and came toward her. He put his hands on her upper arms. "What is it, Emma? You can ask me anything."

"Next Friday, there's a public event where all the finalists present their designs to the press and to the committee. It's semiformal—cocktails, hors d'oeuvres, that kind of thing. I'm allowed to bring a guest."

He raised his brows.

"Would you . . . I mean, can you . . . ?"

"You want me to be your date?"

"Not date!" she said, although that was exactly what she had been hoping. If he wouldn't even take her out to dinner, though, he'd never appear with her at a big to-do like this. "Just as, I don't know, moral support. You must be comfortable with this type of event. You know how they go, whereas I have no clue, and I'm going to be a nervous wreck."

"So you want me to be your security blanket."

"Yes. If you wouldn't mind? And if, you know, you wouldn't mind being out in public with me."

"Why should going out in public be a problem for *me*?" he asked, emphasizing the last word.

What did he mean by that? "I know this is going beyond the bounds of our agreement," she said, "and I don't mean to impose. If anyone asks, you can just say you're my friend. That's true enough, isn't it?"

His expression was unreadable. "True enough. I'm surprised you wouldn't rather take one of your friends. There wouldn't be any hidden undertones with them."

Was he upset? He certainly wasn't delighted by her invitation. "I'll feel less like an outsider with you there," she said, smiling, trying to make it sound like a compliment. "With Daphne, I'd feel like we were teenagers at a dance, afraid to leave each other's side."

A muscle in his jaw worked. She waited, afraid to say anything more, and then he said, "All right. I'll go."

"Thank you."

He didn't seem excited by it, whereas she couldn't think of anyone she'd rather have at her side. He was so supportive of her, and seemed genuinely proud of her accomplishment. However nervous she got when it was time to present her design, she wouldn't be alone. It wouldn't matter if she did well or flubbed up, because either way, he would be there to put his arm around her shoulders when she was finished, to kiss her and tell her "Well done."

At least, that's what she'd thought. Judging from his reaction, it seemed he thought he'd been drafted for a distasteful tour of social duty.

He went to buy the champagne and she finished preparing the meal, but an hour later when they popped the cork and filled their glasses for a toast, Emma felt that the mood had been lost. She felt as if a small distance had opened between them, and she didn't know how to bring them back to where they had been.

They were nibbling at their dessert of seasonal berries in Moscato when she said, "Maybe I shouldn't have asked you to come with me."

He looked at her, his brows raised slightly in question, and waited for her to continue.

"I mean, that type of thing, that's not what we're about."

"No," he said after a long moment. "It's not."

"So I'm sorry I imposed on you like that. It's like the hockey thing—I sometimes forget the limits."

"You'd rather I didn't go, then?"

"I'd love for you to come. But only if you're comfortable."

"If it will help you, then I'd love to come."

Where had all this awkwardness come from? They were talking to each other like strangers, and a small sadness opened up inside Emma. She sensed that she was now on the cusp of a change in her life, and she didn't know if her relationship with Russ would survive it. Their being together had only been to meet present needs, nothing more.

Now her needs were about to change.

They were both subdued the rest of the evening, although Emma tried to talk with enthusiasm about the upcoming event. Every word she said, though, seemed to drain their energy further. The sex was perfunctory, though physically satisfying. Russ left earlier than usual, claiming an early morning meeting, and then Emma was alone again in her apartment.

His apartment, she corrected herself as she tidied up the kitchen. Would she want to stay here if she no longer had Russ in her life? No, it would be too painful, not to mention awkward.

She looked at the room, with her make-do college furniture and cheaply done efforts at comfort and hominess. She'd made the best of what she had, and had begun to think of it as home, as her own space. With the phone call tonight, though, she felt the first hint of disengagement.

Realistically, her chances of winning the contest were slim to none. But being a finalist meant her chances of getting a job had just gone up. And perhaps even more important, she'd found confidence in her own talents and had that confidence validated by others. The Emma who went to interviews now would be a far different creature from the one who'd gone in a month ago. She would be Super Emma, the Emma of her own dreams for herself.

Super Emma wouldn't need or want to be a man's paid mistress, however much she was coming to adore that man. Super Emma would pay her own rent.

A tingle at the end of her nose and a stinging in her eyes warned of the loss that was soon to come. She couldn't ever tell anyone the agreement she and Russ had had; they'd never understand. And she'd also have to keep secret how much she had enjoyed her role, until it became too small for her dreams.

She wiped a tear away with the back of her hand and finished cleaning up.

Sixteen

A re you sure I look okay?" Emma asked for the fifth time.

"I promise, you look great." Russ took his eyes off the traffic long enough to glance over at her, his gaze running over her face and neckline. "More than great."

"It's not too sexy, is it? I don't want to look unprofessional."

"Relax, Emma. You look beautiful."

Emma nibbled at the inside of her lip and looked out the car window, trying to ignore the roiling of her gut. Her dress was a dark green satin underslip covered by a transparent black cheongsam; her shoes had three-and-a-half-inch heels meant to make her feel powerful and tall, although all she could think now was that they didn't fit perfectly and might cause her to stumble and embarrass herself.

The presentation of the finalists' plans for the train station was to take place at a convention center on the waterfront. It wasn't far from her apartment, but Russ had insisted that they drive so that she could arrive fresh. She wished they had walked so that her nervous energy had someplace to go, even though a hike down steep streets in high heels on a windy evening would have left her sweaty and disheveled.

"Oh God, I'm going to be sick," she moaned.

Russ hit the brakes. "Truly?"

She shook her head. "Keep going. I'll save it for the ladies' room."

"Are you really this nervous?"

"Yes! Don't you have any words of advice for me? Imagining people in their underwear, being myself, blah blah blah?"

"Would that help?"

"No. And I shouldn't have worn satin. My sweat is going to show. Big dark green patches of sweat."

He chuckled. "You're going to be fine."

"I don't know how to talk in front of people. I nearly passed out each time I had to present something in school."

"Do you like your design?"

Emma reviewed the plan in her head, trying to see it objectively but feeling instead a reburgeoning of the excitement that had consumed her when the concept first came to her. "It's the best thing I've ever done." Doubt stuck its finger into her joy: "But my best is light-years behind what the others will have done."

"Maybe. Maybe not. But so what? You're a finalist. You've already proven yourself. It doesn't matter what other people did: all that matters is that you communicate to the audience your own belief in your design, and your excitement about it. Explain it to them so they can see it through your own eyes. That's all you have to do, and the only thing worth worrying about."

Emma gnawed a hangnail. "That'll work?"

"If it doesn't, who cares? You've proven yourself, Emma. You don't need to try to impress anyone; you've done that already."

"Have I impressed you?"

He took his eyes off the road long enough to meet hers. "You know you have. I envy your talent. Looking at your design makes me wish I had that type of creative talent. For anything."

The compliment rested uncomfortably on Emma. "But you're creative. You built a whole company, for heaven's sake!"

He shook his head and turned into the parking garage for the conference center. "It's a different type of creativity. Regardless, you almost make me wish I was back at the beginning, trying to get it started. I know you're full of uncertainty, Emma, but that's part of the excitement. Don't fear uncertainty: see it at as the world of possibilities that it truly is. You have everything in front of you—enjoy the journey."

Emma stared at him, her concern for herself forgotten. "Jeez, Russ, you make it sound like you're too old to do something new yourself. You're only thirty-six! If you want to start a new company or try something different, why don't you? You've got enough money to take time off and do what you want, don't you?"

Russ parked the car, then sat silent, staring forward.

"Couldn't you do that?" Emma asked.

"Do you know, I've never seriously thought about it."

"Well, think about it!"

He reached over and grabbed her hand, giving it a squeeze. "Not tonight. Tonight is your night. Let's go show them who you are."

Emma grinned. "Hoo rah! Super Emma has entered the building!"

He raised a brow.

She laughed. "C'mon, coach. Game time."

Russ watched with pride and a strange sense of distance as Emma schmoozed with city officials, railroad reps, and architects. She'd given her presentation with only a few quavers of the voice, finding her footing once she started explaining her concept for the train station. Hers was not the flashiest, most expensive display, but in Russ's eyes it looked to be one of the best. There was a pleasing cohesiveness to her design, each detail, angle, and curve feeling as if it was an inevitable choice that was meant to be. It was satisfying. It was right. It was probably more innovative than the city would go for, but genius shone through her design.

Emma met his eyes across the crowd of people. He smiled and gave her thumbs-up, encouraging her to keep schmoozing. She smiled back, her eyes sparkling, her cheeks flushed.

She was beautiful, full of confidence and joy, at long last stepping into the life she'd been seeking.

A stabbing sense of loss hit him, making him clench his jaw against the sudden, unexpected pain.

It was time to let her go.

Seventeen

Emma pulled off her high heels and tossed them onto the futon. "I was brilliant!" She twirled in the middle of the apartment. "Wasn't I? You can't deny it! Three business cards, I got! Lookee, three!" She stopped spinning and waved her three fingers at Russ. "They all want to talk to me about a job!"

"You were amazing," Russ said.

Emma heard something in his voice and a frown pulled between her brows. "You okay?"

He sighed, and Emma felt a twinge of apprehension as he sat on the futon, moving her shoes to the floor and patting the space beside him in invitation. "We need to talk."

Emma's heart dropped into her stomach. They were not the words that anyone in a relationship wanted to hear. "About what?" she asked, wary, not moving any closer to the futon, as if staying away from it could prevent him from saying what he was about to.

He patted the space next to him again. "It's not bad. Come, sit down."

After looking him over with a suspicious eye, Emma sat down gingerly on the edge of the futon. "What is it?"

He took her hand between his own, and for a moment Emma's heart fluttered. Was he going to propose?

He sighed again, and rubbed the back of her hand. Emma's fluttering thoughts landed back on the ground. Proposals didn't start with heavy sighs.

She wrapped her fingers around his and squeezed. "What is it, Russ?" she asked more softly.

"Emma, these past weeks have been some of the most surprising and memorable of my life. They've been an utter delight, and I don't just mean the sexual aspect."

"But?" she filled in.

"But your life is moving on now. You're soon going to have the job you've been seeking for so long, and when that time comes, I think you should focus on it entirely. I think we'll need to end our arrangement."

A dark coldness spread in her chest. She'd thought the same thing, but hearing it from his own lips made it real, and that reality hurt.

"You said that you didn't have anything bad to say," she said. "You lied."

He wrapped his arm around her and pulled her against him, leaning back until they were snuggled together on the futon. His hand stroked her back. "Oh, Emma. Change is never easy, nor in this case is it bad. You're achieving your dreams, you're stepping into the life you've planned for years. How can that be bad?"

She felt tears tighten her throat. It was on the tip of her tongue to say, "Because I've fallen in love with you." But if he felt as she did, then he would have to say the words first. "Do you know, when I first blathered to you about thinking it would be great to be a man's mistress, I didn't really mean it. I didn't think it was something I would ever have the nerve to do."

His hand on her back stopped its stroking. "Then why did you agree?"

She laughed softly, the sound thick with unshed tears. "Because I was horny and you're cute and I kind of liked you, even though I didn't think you were at all my type. I was shocked when you asked me, you know. I really hadn't figured you for that type of guy."

A laugh rumbled in his chest, and he squeezed her. "What a pair. It's a miracle this ever happened. That day that we agreed to this arrangement, I wasn't even asking you to be my mistress. I'd meant to ask you to be my cook. The conversation was almost over before I realized you'd misunderstood me."

Emma pushed away from him so she could see his face. "You're kidding."

He shook his head.

Emma felt nothing but surprise, and then a trickle of embarrassment started, turning quickly to a flood of humiliation. She covered her face with her hands. "Oh God! Oh God, oh God." A thought struck her, and she dropped her hands, glaring at him. "Why did you agree to it, once you figured out what I'd been thinking?"

"I didn't want to embarrass you. I was going to pretend I'd changed my mind and call it off."

"But you didn't. Why not?"

"Because you'd already agreed, and I couldn't resist the temptation. I found you . . . intensely attractive, and I liked you, even while thinking you were completely not my type."

"So when you asked for something big on Fridays to carry you through the weekend—"

"I meant a casserole."

Emma slowly closed her eyes. She had sold herself to him for money, when that had never been his intention. And in so doing, she had sold away her chance to have a normal relationship with him.

She hadn't cared about that at the time. But now, looking into the future, she saw what a vast distance lay between where she was now and where she might have been if she hadn't jumped to conclusions, and if Russ had been clearer in his word choice. He might have seen her as a potential partner for life, if she hadn't insisted he see her as paid sexual entertainment.

"Emma?"

She opened her eyes and tried to smile. "I want to be mad at you, but I know I have myself to blame."

"I shouldn't have told you."

She shook her head. "It's a lesson I won't forget."

"Emma, I'm sorry. I shouldn't have gone through with it. I never would have, if I'd suspected you would feel this way! But you seemed so eager."

Emma looked down at her hands. She *had* been eager, and up until this moment she hadn't regretted it. If she'd been his cook instead of his mistress, she likely wouldn't have gotten to know him as well as she had. She might not have fallen for him, and it was doubtful he would have made a move on her. They would never have slept together and she would never have discovered as much about herself as she had. Without Russ, she wouldn't have broken free of her own limits and come up with the train station plan.

She met his eyes. "I don't regret it. I know we have to stop when I get a job; I know it's time to move on. But I don't regret what we've done together. Somehow, I think it's exactly what I needed."

"No regrets?"

She shook her head. "Not if we can end on good terms." She meant to say "end as friends," but he might choose to be no more to her than an acquaintance.

The thought almost broke her heart.

She brushed the back of her fingers across his cheek, then stroked the side of his neck. "But I don't have a job yet," she said suggestively, and pulled him to his feet.

"Are you sure?" he asked.

She stood on tiptoe and wrapped her arms around his neck. She brushed her lips against his. "No job at all."

His lips met hers, tenderly. She closed her eyes against his gentleness, so much harder to withstand than brute animal hunger.

"Emma," he whispered against her lips, "What am I going to do without you?"

"Suffer terribly," she said, and kissed him again.

They moved together to her bedroom, stripping the clothes from each other in well-practiced moves. Naked, they slid beneath the sheets and lay on their sides, facing each other.

Emma traced Russ's features with her fingertip, his face expressionless, his eyes watching her every move. When her fingertips trailed away he took the lead, his hand stroking over her body in slow motions, finding the dip of her waist, the hill of her hip, the rise of her breast. She rolled onto her back and he continued his exploration. It was as if they were trying to memorize each other; to form an image that was lodged in the nerves of their fingertips as well as their brains.

Emma closed her eyes when he touched her between her thighs. She parted her legs for him, then felt his mouth move down her torso to replace his hand. He settled between her thighs and lay his warm mouth against her folds, his tongue flicking out to exactly the right spot, in the feather-light touch she'd taught him to use.

There was no embarrassment left in her, no desire to

hold back, no guilt over receiving without giving. She gave herself over to the sensations he created, feeling the wetness of his mouth merge with her own flowing warmth.

"Now," she whispered, reaching down and touching his hair. "Now." She was near to climaxing, and wanted him inside when she did.

He moved up her body, poised above her now on his elbows. She reached between them to guide him to her, lifting her hips against him to lodge him in her opening. She moved both hands to his shoulders and met his eyes.

He looked down at her, his expression still inscrutable, and slowly thrust inside her. She raised her knees and hooked her feet behind him, drawing him deeply inside her.

The tension of pleasure tightened his face and he closed his eyes. Emma slid her arms up around his chest and pulled him close, letting him put his weight on her. His thrusts shook the bed, the brass creaking in an unmistakable rhythm.

Emma felt her own sexual excitement plateau as he thrust, his face against the side of her head, his breath hot in her hair. She felt the satisfaction of being beneath him, his thick cock filling her, but it wasn't a pleasure that would bring her to orgasm.

Russ slowed, and lifted himself off her enough to see her face. Still embedded deep inside her, he slowly kissed her. The tip of his tongue traced the line where her lips met, then parted them and sucked on her lower lip.

His hips thrust once, slow and deep.

Emma's eyes closed, her back arching in pleasure.

Russ teased her mouth open, dipping his tongue inside, rubbing against her own. She felt the rough warmth and instinctively sucked on it, just as she would suck on his cock.

His pelvis moved with slow strength, his cock stroking inside her with careful deliberation, as if making certain that each millimeter of her passage knew that he was there and could feel the shape of him.

He thrust his tongue against hers, matching the rhythm to his hips, his movements agonizingly slow and careful. Emma felt her hunger for him grow anew, and she rocked her hips against him and sucked furiously at his tongue.

Russ grasped her hip with one hand and held her still, forcing her to accept the agonizingly slow motions.

Emma could stand only one thrust more, and before he was seated to the hilt she felt herself tip over the edge, orgasm throbbing through her. She could feel him moving back against her G-spot, could feel the clenching muscles at her opening try to grip him, could feel the pull of his movement against the hood of her clitoris.

"Russ," she cried softly, "Russ, I can't stop."

He thrust once more, quickly, and then she heard the moan deep in his throat and felt the pulse of his own orgasm join hers. His body was hard as stone, pinning her in place. As he held motionless inside her she felt her own waves gradually die down, and then he settled upon her, his weight nearly taking the breath from her, his face settling beside hers.

A moment later she heard the soft snort of his snore.

Emma felt tears trickle from the corners of her eyes, seeping down into her hair. They might have sex a time or two more, but in her heart she knew that tonight was the beginning of good-bye.

Eighteen

Emma violently speared a clam on her fork and ate it, chewing viciously.

"What is it?" Russ asked. "Emma, you've been quiet all evening. What's bothering you?" There had been a quiet tension to their nights together since the contest event two weeks ago, but nothing like this. Emma had been subdued since his arrival. He'd tried to give her time to say what was bothering her, but plainly this was one of those times that she needed to be asked.

Emma speared another clam, then dropped her fork onto her plate and her face into her hands.

"Emma?"

"I'm okay," she mumbled, and heaved a heavy sigh. She dropped her hands, her eyes shimmering with unshed tears. "I was offered a job today."

Russ's gut sank to the floor. So soon? He'd thought they'd

have a month more, at least. "Which firm?" he asked hoarsely.

"Mary Beeton and Associates. It's smallish, but I like her and I think I'll learn a lot from her and her staff. I won't be an anonymous intern doing grunt work. I'll be a known intern doing grunt work."

"Congratulations."

Emma's mouth turned down at the corners. "I should be happy. I *am* happy. Happy happy happy. Wee hee, look at me."

"I wish you'd told me sooner. We could have gone out to celebrate."

Emma plunked her elbows on the table and covered her eyes with her hands. "I don't want to celebrate. I want . . ."

His heart thumped. "You want . . ."

"More time." She dropped her hands and looked at him hopefully. "We could have a little more time, couldn't we? I don't start for a week."

A reprieve. Did she find it as hard to contemplate goodbye as he did?

Might she possibly want more from him than this? Tonight was his last chance to find out. "Emma—"

The door intercom buzzed, interrupting him.

"Were you expecting someone?" he asked.

She shook her head. "Maybe they buzzed the wrong apartment."

It buzzed again.

Scowling, Emma rose and headed to the door.

Should he even ask his question or was it unfair?

"Hello?" Emma said into the intercom.

Russ couldn't make out the response, distorted by the electronics, but after a quick, helpless glance at him, Emma buzzed the caller in downstairs.

"I'm so sorry," she said, her hands clasped and distress on her brow. "It's Daphne. Her boyfriend kicked her out. I told her I'd always be here if she needed me . . ."

"You don't have to apologize," he said, silently consigning Daphne to the lower reaches of hell. "I understand."

"What were you going to say to me, before she interrupted?"

He shook his head. "I should go," he said, standing. "Daphne will need you to herself."

"Russ," Emma said, grasping his arm. "Don't go. Not yet. This can't be good-bye, not like this. I'll settle her in and then . . . maybe we can go for a walk or something."

The door buzzed.

"Stay?" Emma pleaded. "Please?"

He couldn't refuse the look in her eyes. He nodded.

Emma dashed to the door.

There was a fluster of female drama in the foyer and he waited it out, his discomfort rising with each weepy, high-pitched sound from the unseen Daphne.

The hysterical voice was suddenly silent. Russ turned around and saw Daphne in the living room.

"Daphne, you remember Russ," Emma said.

"Of course."

Russ held out his hand. "Nice to see you again."

As if automated, Daphne shook it. She turned to Emma. "Am I interrupting? I'm interrupting, aren't I?" She looked around the apartment and noticed the table with its half-eaten meal. "Oh God, you were having dinner." Her expression became panicked and she backed toward the door, her hands waving in apology. "Emma, I'm sorry, I'm ruining your date with all my private garbage!"

"Don't be silly," Emma said. "Sit down, will you? Are you hungry? Would you like some wine?"

Daphne looked again at Russ.

"Please, stay," he said, knowing he could say nothing else.

"Are you sure?"

He nodded.

Daphne's lower lip trembled.

"Wine?" Russ asked quickly, hoping to forestall the incipient emotional outpouring.

Daphne nodded, looking miserable, and plopped down onto the futon.

Glad to have something to do, Russ headed to the kitchen for a fresh glass.

Then someone knocked on the apartment door.

Russ halted, not sure he'd heard it.

The knocking came again, more firm. "Emma?" a man asked.

Russ turned around and met Emma's eyes. She shrugged

and shook her head. "Maybe it's Derek? Daphne, did you tell Derek where you were going?"

"No!" Daphne squeaked. "I hope he thinks I got run over by a truck and am lying on a highway somewhere, and that he'll feel guilty about it for the rest of his life."

The knocking came again.

Russ, could you get it?" Emma asked, wrapping her arms around Daphne, who promptly fell blubbering onto Emma's chest.

Maybe he could make an escape while he was at it. He went to the door and pulled it open.

Kevin stood staring at him.

"Kevin! What the— What are you doing here?" Russ asked in surprise.

"I'm confirming my suspicions—that's what I'm doing here!"

Oh, shit. "Which suspicions were those?" he asked coolly.

"Fuck off, Russ." Kevin pushed past him into the apartment, and was brought up short at sight of Emma and Daphne on the futon.

"Kevin? What are you doing here? How did you know I lived here?" Emma asked in surprise.

Daphne's face appeared over Emma's shoulder, eyes and nose red, hair mussed. "Christ! Who's here now?"

"I—" Kevin started.

Daphne huffed out an angry breath and got up, dashing for the bathroom, casting an evil glare at Kevin.

"I didn't mean . . . ," he said to Emma.

Emma shook her head and stood. "Bad timing. I really prefer to be phoned before someone drops by, if you don't mind. How'd you get in the building?"

"I followed behind someone. I wasn't sure you lived here; it was just a hunch. I had to see for myself."

"See what for yourself?"

Kevin looked from her to Russ. "Had to see that my *friend* had betrayed me in the worst possible way."

Anger and guilt stormed within Russ, with no answer he could give. The truth was so much worse than even Kevin could guess.

"Russ, you *knew* I felt something for Emma," he went on. "So why's she living in your apartment? You're the guy she said she was seeing, aren't you? You couldn't tell me that? If you were going to screw me, the least you could do was be honest about it. Did you think I couldn't handle it if she preferred you to me?"

"I didn't want him to tell you," Emma said, stepping forward. "I didn't want to come between you two, since I knew that this wasn't going to last."

Kevin pulled his chin in, looking at Emma. "Not going to last?"

"I wanted a fling, and he was convenient."

Her words, spoken so harshly to Kevin, confirmed what Russ had been trying to deny: that the foundation of their relationship was flawed. To build anything upon it was to invite ruin.

Kevin's face fell as he took in Emma's words. "But . . . if that's what you wanted, why wasn't I good enough?"

Emma smiled sadly. "Because you wanted something more that I would never be able to give. Knowing how you thought of me, how could I let Russ tell you that he was having sex with me, with no intention of a more serious relationship? You would have hated him, when it was me you should have hated, for seducing your friend. I'm the one you should be mad at, not Russ."

Kevin scowled, looking back at him. "You didn't have to take her up on the offer!"

"I shouldn't have," Russ said. "I was weak."

"Goddamn it! I expected more from you, you with your careful morals. You're a fucking hypocrite, you know that?"

Russ's jaw tightened against Kevin's disappointment. "I have flaws like everyone else."

"You do a fricking good job of making people think you don't."

"Oh, shut up, will you?" Daphne said, emerging from the bathroom and glaring at Kevin, her red-rimmed eyes and flyaway hair adding satanic fervor to her words. "You're just pissed because he got to screw her and you didn't."

"Who are you?"

"The only person here who's not trying to spare your

candy-ass feelings. You knew you didn't stand a chance with Emma, so what did you do? Started stalking her. You're a sicko, you know that? You ought to be locked up."

"I didn't *stalk* her!" Kevin protested.

"Then what are you doing here?" Daphne shot back, plainly glad to have found a male target for her angst. "Christ, it's no wonder she didn't want to go out with you. She oughta get a restraining order!"

"Where do you get off—"

"Kevin!" Russ interrupted. "Maybe it's time to go."

Daphne narrowed her eyes at Kevin, then plopped onto the futon and crossed her arms over her chest. "I think it's time you left, stalker-boy."

Russ grabbed Kevin's arm and dragged him toward the door, explaining beneath his breath. "Her boyfriend just kicked her out. Leave her alone."

Kevin looked back for one last glimpse at Daphne before Russ forced him out into the hallway. "She was dumped?" Kevin asked after the door closed.

Russ nodded.

"But she's hot. Why would anyone dump her?"

Russ looked at Kevin in disbelief, seeing the softening in Kevin's eyes, the burgeoning empathy. "Kevin. No. Don't go there."

"She needs someone who'll treat her better. That's why she was acting like that. She needs to be loved."

Russ rolled his eyes. "I'll have Emma give her your number."

Kevin blinked. "Thanks."

"*Oh for Christ's sake,*" Russ said under his breath. "Go home, Kevin, will you?"

"You won't forget to tell Emma?"

"Go home."

Russ watched him disappear, then turned and found Emma had opened the door and was gazing at him. She stepped out into the hall, the door snicking shut behind her.

"This isn't how I imagined our last night together would go," she said. "We can't end it this way, can we? Shouldn't we go another week?"

He shook his head reluctantly, feeling an emptiness akin to when his brother had died. "We both know it's over. It would only ruin our memories, to drag it out. Good-byes should be short and sweet."

"But to end like this . . ."

"Our moment together is past. You know it." He gestured at the apartment behind her, and the unseen Daphne.

Her mouth was unhappy. "I don't like good-byes," she whispered.

He cupped her face between his hands, not trusting himself to hold her closer than that. "We'll see each other again, Emma," he said softly. "A year or two from now, we'll have lunch, we'll catch up. I'll hear how your career is progressing. You'll hear how boring mine still is."

"I don't want to face a year without you."

He pressed his forehead against hers, feeling the sting of tears in his eyes, the tightness of them in his throat. "Me neither."

"Then why?"

He raised his head and saw tears spilling down her cheeks. He pressed a kiss to her forehead, closing his eyes for a long moment, breathing in the scent of her. "Because I'm in love with you," he whispered against her skin. "And it will hurt too much to see you."

He felt her stiffen in his arms. She pulled back, looking up at him. "You *love* me?"

"I tried not to."

She shook her head. "You idiot."

"I shouldn't have told you," he said, regretting it.

She laughed and wrapped her arms around his neck. "But Russ, couldn't you tell? I'm in love with you, too. Head over heels, hopelessly in love."

With her words, the bands of grief around his heart shattered. He held her close, and for the first time in years knew what it was to feel joy.

Nineteen

He's so quiet," Emma said, looking down at baby Wade sleeping on her chest. "He's like a turtle on a log."

"You should hear him when he's hungry," Beth said, sitting back in her lounge chair and picking up her glass of lemonade. It was almost the summer solstice, and for once, the weather had lived up to the calendar and given them a balmy day. "It's just like a boy to yell when he's hungry, yell when he's tired, yell when he poops. I'll bet girls are quieter."

"Do you think you'll be trying for a girl?" Emma asked.

"Oh, I don't know: people say boys are easier. Can you imagine dealing with a daughter during puberty? I can barely handle Daphne."

Emma choked on her lemonade. "She seems much happier now!"

"Since she got Kevin as her doormat."

"Maybe she really likes him."

Beth snorted. "No, he'd make an adoring husband, so therefore she won't marry him. Although she probably should."

Beth's husband, Ty, opened the screen slider from the kitchen and came out with a tray of hot dogs. "Ladies, prepared to be astounded. The chef is about to fire up the grill."

Emma grinned.

"No fireballs this time," Beth said. "You nearly burned down the neighborhood last time."

Ty bent over the back of her chair and kissed the top of her head. "Have faith. Your man is mastering fire for you! He is cooking meat!"

"Or a reasonable facsimile thereof." Beth smiled as Ty strolled to the far end of the patio.

"Things are good between you?" Emma asked softly.

Beth met her eyes. "Yeah, things are good. He's a pain in the ass half the time, but he's a good man." Her eyes went to baby Wade. "Better than I expected." She flashed Emma a grin. "I remember what a mess *I* was during my pregnancy, and he put up with me. That all feels like a lifetime ago, in some ways."

"It does to me, too. Big changes do that, I guess."

"So how's the train station going?" Beth asked. "When are they actually going to start construction?"

Emma laughed. "Five years? Never? Who knows!"

Beyond all her expectations, her design had been chosen for the new station. She was too inexperienced to be in charge of the project and was treated more as a half-forgotten consultant than as the architect, but the fact remained that it was her design concept that was going to be the inspiration for the new King Street Station. Someday.

At the far end of the patio, a *whoosh* went up and the tin hot dog tray clattered to the cement.

"Ty?" Beth cried.

A string of curse words flowed upon the summer air, ending with, "Goddamn piece of crap."

Emma saw Ty scooping hot dogs off the patio, wiping some of them off on his shorts.

"Pretend you didn't see that," Beth said. "The grill will burn off any germs, and he'll be hurt if you don't eat one."

Emma smiled weakly.

They sat listening to Ty work, and watched the baby sleep.

"So have you slept with him yet? I mean again. I mean—"

"I know what you mean," Emma said, laughing. Russ, for strange reasons of honor that did not entirely make sense to her, had insisted that they date like "a normal couple" for three months before they had sex again. Emma's protest that normal couples didn't usually wait three months was met with a set jaw.

"I never heard of a guy saying that sex had come too soon, and he wanted to backtrack to the wooing stage."

"He's unique, all right. But I don't plan on waiting another whole month for sex. I'm going to break his will tomorrow."

"How?"

Emma grinned. "Ever hear of a French maid?"

Russ strapped on his bicycle helmet with its fronds of kale wedged into the openings.

"You're not really wearing that, are you?" Greg asked.

"The helmet?"

Greg gave him a look. "You're buck naked, and you feel the need to put on a hat?"

"Safety first."

"I can't believe you talked me into this," Greg said.

"All you're doing is standing there—you're not riding."

"Tina would never forgive me displaying my manly goods to the eyes of other women. And quite frankly, I've seen more of *your* manly goods than I need to for a lifetime."

"I'm painted green from head to toe, and I have kale tied over my crotch."

"I've still seen too much." Greg pulled a digital camera out of his pocket. "Gotta show Tina, when she gets back from her trip."

"Like hell you will!"

"She's always liked you. This way I can show her that she got the better package with me."

"Oh, for God's sake."

"Lift your kale and smile!" Greg snapped a picture, then examined the result on the small screen. "You look like a piece of broccoli." He held the camera out for Russ to see.

Russ saw himself scowling out of the small screen, looking like a mental ward escapee. "Jesus."

They moved toward the other riders gathering in preparation for the annual Fremont Solstice Parade, Russ walking his bike.

"What are you supposed to be, again?" Greg asked.

"The Green Man. An ancient mythological figure, usually associated with death, rebirth, and fertility."

"You're having a midlife crisis, aren't you?"

"I'm only thirty-seven. I'm not old enough for that."

"Then why the hell come out here with these freaks?"

A young man on an ape-hanger bicycle, wearing nothing but a black vest and helmet, gave Greg a dirty look.

"Present company excepted," Greg said.

Russ smiled. "Because I can."

Greg threw up his hands. "Fine! But you didn't have to drag me along."

"Sure I did. I needed someone to take my clothes. My cell phone's in the side pocket, by the way." He nodded at the carry-on bag Greg held.

"Why couldn't Emma have done this?"

"She's waiting at the end of the parade route, with a bathrobe. Hey, is my butt still green? Does it need a touch-up?"

Greg pulled back as if from roadkill. "I'm not touching you."

Russ laughed.

The crowd of riders, nearly three hundred strong, began to form into a column, waiting for the whistle that would mark the start of the parade.

Russ threw his leg over his bike. "Wish me luck!"

"You don't need luck," said a dark-haired, masked young woman, riding up and stopping between Russ and Greg. Her body was painted black and white, to look as if she was wearing a French maid's outfit. There were white ruffles around her painted neckline, cuffs, and midthigh hem, and a white apron painted over her lower belly. A small white cap sat atop her head. "You have me!"

"*Emma?*" Russ choked out.

The whistle blew. The column of riders let out a cheer and began to move, Emma along with them. White apron ties painted over her toned, black-painted buttocks rippled with movement as she pedaled.

"You lucky bastard," Greg said.

Russ grinned and joined the throng, quickly catching up to Emma. And together they cruised down the street, nothing but the wind between their naked skin and the hard road below—and nothing but possibilities ahead.